GREAT ILLUSTRATED CLASSICS

KING SOLOMON'S MINES

H. Rider Haggard

adapted by
Jack Kelly

Illustrations by Pablo Marcos

BARONET
B O O K S

GREAT ILLUSTRATED CLASSICS

edited by
Joshua E. Hanft and Rochelle Larkin

Contents

About the Author

H. Rider Haggard was born in England in 1856. He had five older brothers and four sisters. His father, a country gentleman, was strict with his children.

Rider was a quiet boy who never liked school and didn't do well at his studies. But he did like to read. *Robinson Crusoe* was his favorite book, along with *The Three Musketeers*, and Dickens' *A Tale of Two Cities*.

As a tall, thin young man of fourteen, Rider sailed to South Africa as a government clerk. It was a time when England had colonies around the world.

After a few years, Rider quit his job and began to raise ostriches. When he was 24 he returned to England and married his wife Louisa. They had a son, Jock, and three daughters.

Rider wrote novels about his experiences in

Africa. In those days, parts of Africa had not been explored and were very mysterious.

Haggard became a lawyer, but his novels brought him fame and fortune. Robert Louis Stevenson had just written *Treasure Island*. Rider also wanted to publish an adventure for boys, so in 1885 he wrote *King Solomon's Mines*. It was very popular.

Rider traveled to lands over the world, including Egypt and Iceland. While he and Louisa were in Mexico looking for ancient treasure, they found out that 10-year-old Jock had died from measles. His son's death hurt Rider very deeply.

In America, Haggard met Teddy Roosevelt. Back home in England he worked with the government to help solve farm problems. He wrote many more novels, a total of 34. Most were set in foreign lands and told of gripping adventures.

H. Rider Haggard died in 1925 at the age of 69.

I Met Two Men on the Ship.

CHAPTER 1

The Legend of Solomon's Mines

I first met Sir Henry Curtis and Captain John Good on a ship that was sailing along the coast of South Africa. I was returning home after some bad luck on an elephant hunt beyond Bamangwato. Everything went wrong that trip. Plus, I came down with a fever. I wasn't so young anymore and I needed to take time off and rest.

I was sailing toward my home in Durban, farther to the north. I got to talking with the two men on the ship. The first, Sir Henry, was a tall, well-built man of about thirty. He had blond hair and a thick blond beard and deep-set gray eyes. He reminded me strongly of somebody else, but I couldn't remember who it was.

I knew right away that the second man was a naval officer. Captain Good was about the same age as his friend, but short and stout. He had dark hair and was clean-shaven. Something about the way he moved around on the ship told me he had been at sea a great deal. He always wore a monocle clenched in his right eye socket and had a beautiful set of false teeth!

"You're Allan Quatermain, aren't you?" Sir Henry Curtis asked as the three of us sat down at dinner.

I said I was.

Not much more was said at dinner, but afterwards Sir Henry invited me back to his cabin to talk.

"You were in Bamangwato two years ago, weren't you?" Curtis asked.

At Sea a Great Deal

"I was," I answered, surprised that he would know so much about me.

"Did you happen to meet a man named Neville there?"

"Yes," I said. "He left to go into the interior with a guide named Jim. He was going to go as far back as any man had ever gone, he said. Why are you interested?"

"Mr. Neville is my brother," Sir Henry said.

He went on to explain that he and his younger brother George had been very close until a few years ago. Then they had quarrelled bitterly. When their father died, Sir Henry kept the inheritance for himself. George became angry and went off to Africa. He took the name Neville and hoped to make his fortune in the wild. Sir Henry regretted his own actions very much and wrote to George, but the letters never reached him.

"George is the only relation I have," Sir Henry said. "As time went on I became more and more anxious to know if he was dead or alive. I asked people. They mentioned that he had gone to the interior and had met you. I decided to come here myself from England and try to find him. Captain Good was kind enough to come with me. I would give anything to know that my brother is safe."

"I can understand your concern," I told him. "I have a son, Harry. He's in England studying to be a doctor. I don't know what I would do if he became lost."

"You've been out here a long time, haven't you, Mr. Quatermain?" Captain Good asked.

"Many years," I said.

"Do you know why my brother was going into the interior?" Sir Henry asked.

"Yes," I said, "but I've never told anyone. He was starting out to find King Solomon's Mines."

"Solomon's Mines!" they both said. "Where are they?"

"I don't know," I replied. "I know where they are said to be. I once saw the peaks of the mountains that border them. But there were a hundred and thirty miles of desert in between.

"Promise Not to Reveal . . ."

Only one man that I know of has ever crossed there."

"Tell us what you've heard," Sir Henry said.

"I will, but only if you both promise not to reveal anything that I tell you."

"Certainly," they both said.

I told them that years ago I had heard about spectacular ruins that exist in those remote and wild lands. The Suliman Mountains, I was told, were especially interesting.

"Why were they so interesting?" Captain Good asked.

"Suliman is Arabic for Solomon," I said. "This could have been the place where King Solomon got his fabulous wealth."

I told them that beyond the Suliman Mountains lived a tribe of peoples related to the Zulus, but even taller. There lived among them great wizards who knew the secrets of the "bright stones" that were dug out of a mine there. I had laughed at these tales at the time. But later, when diamonds were discovered in South Africa, I began to wonder.

"But King Solomon's Mines could be any-where," Sir Henry said. "How would anyone ever find them?"

"Wait," I said. "I haven't gotten to the strangest part of all."

Some years ago, I told them, I was hunting back in the countryside. I had become very ill with a fever and could hardly get out of bed. I met a Portuguese trader, a very polite gentle-man. He was tall and thin, with dark eyes and a curling mustache. His name was Jose Sil-vestre. We became friendly. When he left for the interior, he said, 'Good-bye, my friend. If we meet again I will be the richest man in the world.'

I was too weak to laugh at his joke. I watched him head out toward the desert. I wondered if he was mad. What did he think he would possibly find there?

A week later I was feeling better. One evening, as the red sun was sinking into the desert, I saw a man approaching. He must have been a European because he wore a coat.

"The Richest Man in the World."

He staggered, then dropped to his hands and knees. It was Jose Silvestre.

There wasn't much left of him. He was just a skeleton and some skin. His face was yellow with fever. His eyes stood nearly out of his head. His hair had gone white. "Water," he cried. His lips were cracked, his tongue black and swollen. I gave him some water with a little milk in it. He drank two quarts without stopping.

Then the fever took over and he began to rave about Suliman's Mountains and the diamonds and the desert. I did what I could for him, but I knew he was sure to die.

He slept through the night. In the morning the rays of the sun hit the tallest of the Suliman Mountains.

"There it is!" Jose Silvestre said, pointing with his thin arm. "But I will never reach it. No one will!"

I wondered what he meant. "Are you there?" he said. "My eyes grow dark."

"I'm here," I said. "You must rest."

"I'm dying," he said. "You have been good to me. I will give you the papers. Perhaps you will get there if you can live through the desert which has killed me and my servant."

He pulled out a leather pouch and handed it to me. Inside were some papers. "My ancestor came here three hundred years ago," he said. 'He was the first Portuguese to land in Africa. His name was also Jose Silvestre. He died in those mountains. His servant found him and brought back these papers. They have been in my family ever since. Maybe you will succeed where I failed." His mind wandered. In an hour he was dead. "But what was in the papers?" Sir Henry asked.

I said, "I have shown them to no one except my dear wife, who's dead now. She thought it was all nonsense. I made a copy and had the Portuguese translated into English. Part of it was a map. I'll show it to you."

I unfolded the paper. It read:

"I, Jose Silvestre, am now dying of hunger in the cave near the top of the southern peak of

"Blood for Ink . . ."

the mountains called the White Twins, in this year 1590. I am using my own blood for ink to write this. If my servant finds it I have told him to see that it gets to the king. He can send an army to cross the desert and defeat the brave Kukuana tribe. Then he will be able to reach the mines of King Solomon. I have seen the diamonds there in that treasure chamber beyond the Place of Death. Because of Gagool, the witch-finder, I barely escaped alive. Let he who comes follow the great road that Solomon made. Let him kill Gagool. Farewell."

When they finished looking at the papers, both Sir Henry and Captain Good turned to me in astonishment.

"I have been around the world twice," Captain Good said, "but I have never heard a story like that in my life."

"You're not making it up, are you, Mr. Quatermain?" Sir Henry said.

"Do you think I'm one of those silly fellows who thinks it witty to tell lies?" I said. "If you don't believe me, forget it." I stood up to leave.

"No, sit down," Sir Henry said. "I see that you aren't trying to fool us. Only, your story is so very strange."

"I haven't yet told you about your brother," I said.

The morning that Mr. Neville was starting on his journey, I told them, I saw his guide Jim preparing the wagon.

"Where are you off to, Jim?" I asked. "Hunting elephants?"

"No, we are after something more valuable than ivory," he said. "We are going looking for diamonds! We are going to Suliman's Mountains."

"Do you believe that foolish story of Solomon's Mines?"

"Mr. Neville says he must make a fortune somehow. He is determined."

"They started across the desert. That was the last I ever heard of them," I explained.

"I am very afraid," I said to Sir Henry, "that your brother is dead."

"I am aware of that," he said. "But I mean to

They Started Across the Desert.

trace him to those mountains and beyond. I won't give up until I find him, or until I know for sure he's dead. Will you come with me?"

"No, thank you, Sir Henry," I said. "I'm too old for wild-goose chases of that sort. My son depends on me. I cannot afford to risk my life."

Both Sir Henry and Captain Good looked very disappointed.

"Mr. Quatermain," Sir Henry said, "I am very well off. I will pay you as much as you want. Before we leave I will arrange for your son to be taken care of in case anything happens to us. You are our only hope of reaching those mountains and of finding my brother. If we come across any diamonds, they will belong to you and Good."

"That is a most generous offer," I said. "But as this is the most difficult expedition I've ever considered, I would like some time to think it over. I'll give you my answer before the ship reaches Durban."

I said good night and went to bed. That night I dreamed of poor dead Silvestre and of diamonds. Before this shipboard encounter, I had pretty nearly put poor Silvestre and his strange story out of my mind. Now the tale was haunting me, not only in my dreams, but in my waking hours as well. I had to give it much thought.

I had to give Sir Henry my answer, and soon.

We Came Near Durban.

CHAPTER 2

We Meet Umbopa

It took us five days to sail up to Durban. All the time I was thinking over Sir Henry's offer. We did not speak about his brother again. I told them many tales of the hunting trips I had been on. They were all true ones, too. No hunter in that land has to make up exciting stories.

Finally we came near Durban. It was January, which in South Africa is our hottest month. The coast was beautiful, with red sand hills and wide areas of green fields. Sir Henry,

Captain Good and I sat down for our last meal together on the ship.

When we came back on deck, the moon was up. It shined silver off the calm sea and gave everything a feeling of peace.

"Well, Mr. Quatermain," Sir Henry said, "Have you thought about my offer?"

"I hope we can count on you," Captain Good said.

I had been turning over his offer in my mind all that time, but I still hadn't made up my mind. Now, in an instant, I decided.

"Yes, gentlemen," I said, "I will go with you. I have three conditions. First, Sir Henry, you will pay all expenses and Captain Good and I will share in any ivory or other valuables we find. Second, you will pay me five hundred British pounds for my services. I will go with you until you turn back, or until we succeed, or until we meet disaster. Third, in the event I am killed, you will arrange to pay my son Harry two hundred pounds a year for five years."

"I accept your terms gladly," Sir Henry said.

"Or Until We Meet Disaster."

"I would pay even more, considering what you know of the country."

"I like you both and I think we will make a good team," I said. "That's extremely important on a long journey such as this."

"With you along, I'm sure we will succeed," Sir Henry said.

"I don't agree," I had to tell him. "I think it's probable that we won't return alive. The fate of Jose Silvestre and the fate of your brother will be our fate—death."

"Then why do you agree to come?" he asked.

"Mainly I am thinking of my son. I've never made a lot of money, and most hunters don't live long. If I die on a hunting trip, I leave him with nothing. If I die on this journey, I know that he will be taken care of."

"None of us can know what waits ahead," Sir Henry said. "But I can tell you, I am going through to the end, sweet or bitter."

"There will be no turning back," I agreed.

The next day we went ashore at Durban. Sir Henry and Captain Good set up a tent in the yard of my little house and we began to prepare for the expedition.

First we arranged for Sir Henry to have money sent to my boy Harry in case anything happened to us. He also paid me my five hundred pounds in advance. Next we bought a strong wagon and twenty oxen. Sixteen of them would pull the wagon and we would have four extra. These oxen are small but strong and tough. They can live in the wild where bigger oxen can't.

We also packed a box of medicines. We were fortunate that Captain Good had had medical training and was as good as a doctor at treating illnesses. He had a medicine chest and some doctors' instruments. His knowledge would prove very useful to us when we were a long way from civilization.

We took along many other things we would need on a long expedition: pots and pans, a compass, hunting knives, and my bull whip.

Most important were the guns. We took three elephant guns, each weighing fifteen

A Tall and Handsome Zulu

pounds. We also obtained three high-velocity rifles. Those were good for shooting medium-sized game like antelope. We took one double-barrel shotgun for shooting birds and small game, three light Winchester repeating rifles as spare guns, and three Colt revolvers. Every hunter knows how important guns and ammunition are on an expedition.

We took five men with us. They all had to be brave and reliable. Goza and Tom were the Zulus we hired to handle the wagon. We also hired a Hottentot named Ventvogel, who I knew was an excellent tracker, and another Zulu named Khiva, who spoke perfect English.

We still needed one more man. We wondered where we would find someone when a man came to talk to me. He was a tall and handsome Zulu. He wore a loincloth and a necklace of lions' claws. Around his head he had the black ring that is worn by Zulus of high dignity.

"What is your name?" I asked.

"Umbopa," he said.

"What do you want, Umbopa?"

"I hear that you go very far to the north, beyond the Manica country," he said in the Zulu language. "You are taking the white chiefs from over the water. Is this true?"

"Why do you ask where we go?" I said.

"I would like to travel with you."

"Tell me about yourself."

"I am of the Zulu people, but not one of them. My own tribe lives far to the north. I have no home. I have wandered for many years. I came down from the north when I was a child. I left Zululand and came here because I wanted to see the white man's ways. Now I am tired and I want to go home. Here is not my place. I want no money to travel with you. I am a brave man and will earn the meat I will eat."

He did look different than most Zulus. But his offer to come without pay made me suspicious. I translated his words into English for my companions and asked them what they thought.

"He's as big as Sir Henry," Captain Good

"I Have Wandered for Many Years."

said, "and very strong looking."

Sir Henry gazed at the man's proud and handsome face. The two of them were almost the same size, about six feet tall and very strong. "I like your looks, Mr. Umbopa," he said. "I will take you along."

Umbopa must have understood some English. He said, "It is well."

We soon left on our trip of more than a thousand miles.

CHAPTER 3

We March Into the Desert

Our goal was to reach Sitanda Village, a thousand miles north of Durban. It was a journey that would take us almost five months. From there we would begin to cross the desert toward the Suliman Mountains.

For part of the way, we drove our wagon. Often I needed to crack my bull-whip over the heads of the oxen to get them to pull the wagon out of a gully or over a rock.

We reached Inyati, the trading town of the Matabele country. At that point we had to

We Continued on Foot.

leave our wagon and oxen behind, along with the two drivers. Farther on we would meet the dreadful tsetse fly, whose bite kills any animal except for a man or a donkey.

We were encouraged because some of the villagers at Inyati remembered an Englishman named Neville who had sold his wagon there two years ago. He had gone up into the country and never been seen again. We knew we were on the right track.

We continued on our way with Umbopa, Ventvogel, and Khiva, plus a few men we hired to help carry our baggage. We were all quiet as we continued on foot. We wondered if we would ever see that wagon again. I didn't expect we would.

Umbopa, who was marching in front, broke into a Zulu chant about brave men journeying into the wilderness. In his song the land they find is a paradise filled with game. We all laughed at Umbopa's cheerful nature. We had grown to like Umbopa very much.

We had been travelling for many long weeks

now and we looked it. My gray hair had grown out and Sir Henry's blond locks had gotten quite long. The only one who remained clean and tidy was Captain Good. He wore a brown tweed shooting suit with a hat to match. He kept his face clean shaven and his monocle and false teeth in good order. He even wore a clean collar on his shirt. He was the neatest man ever to go into the wilderness.

"I always like to look like a gentleman," he told us.

One night we were sitting around the fire telling stories. Most of our helpers had gone to sleep. Only Umbopa was still up. He was sitting away from the others and must have been thinking about something.

Suddenly we heard a huge roar from the bush.

"That's a lion," I told the others.

Immediately afterward came the loud trumpeting of an elephant. We peered out of our camp and could see the shadowy forms of wild animals moving toward the water hole.

Clean and Tidy Captain Good

The sun was just coming up when we again heard the awful roar. It sounded as if the lion were just outside our camp. I took my rifle and my bull whip and ran out. The others followed.

We turned a corner and there he was, a wild-maned lion who looked at us with bared teeth and gave a low growl. We all stopped dead in our tracks.

Captain Good wanted to shoot the beast, but I stopped him. "It's not necessary to kill him," I said.

"If I don't fire, he may kill us," he said.

"Stay calm and don't move," I said.

I took a step toward the lion, never taking my eyes off him. He was now crouching, ready to leap forward. I could see each of his long, sharp teeth.

"Back!" I shouted. I flicked out my whip and snapped it. The lion swatted at it with his huge paw.

I thought I might have to use my rifle after all, but a few more cracks of the whip made the lion retreat. He slunk off into the bushes.

"He could have killed you," Sir Henry said.

"I knew he had his eye on something juicier than me," I said. I pointed to where a small herd of black sable antelope were watering at the pool.

We started on our way. Late in the afternoon we came across a herd of eland. We didn't need any meat, but Captain Good wanted a closer look at these heavy antelope, which he'd never seen before. He gave Umbopa his rifle and moved closer, followed by Khiva. Sir Henry and I sat down to rest and enjoy the beautiful scenery.

Suddenly we heard an elephant scream. Against the red setting sun we saw the black outline of a charging elephant, its mighty trunk raised high. An instant later we saw Good and Khiva racing full speed back toward us.

It was a huge bull elephant. We lifted our rifles, but we didn't dare to shoot. The elephant was too far away and we were afraid of hitting one of the men.

The Elephant Turned on Khiva.

Captain Good slipped and fell on his face right in front of the elephant. We gave a gasp, for we knew he must die. We ran as hard as we could toward him.

It was all over in a few seconds, but it did not end as we had thought. Khiva, seeing that Good was helpless, turned back and threw his spear at the charging elephant. It struck the beast in his trunk.

With a scream of pain, the elephant turned on the brave Khiva. He lifted the poor man with his trunk, hurled him to the ground, and trampled him to death. Sir Henry and I raised our rifles and fired at the enormous beast again and again. Finally he fell dead.

Good wrung his hands in grief over the courageous man who had saved his life. Umbopa looked down at his fallen comrade and said, "He is dead, but he died like a man."

We journeyed on for many more hard weeks before we reached Sitanda's Village, the real starting-point of our expedition. This was a small settlement by a river with some fields where the people kept cattle and grew crops. It was the end of fertile land. Everything beyond was dry sand.

That evening Sir Henry and I walked to the top of a slope to look at what lay before us. In the far distance we could make out the blue outline of the Suliman mountains and their white caps of snow.

"There is where Solomon's Mines are located," I said. "Who knows if we'll ever make it."

"My brother should be there," he said. "If he is, I'll reach him somehow."

"I hope so," I said. As we turned back toward the village we found that Umbopa had followed us. He also gazed across the wilderness.

"Is that where you plan to go?" he asked in Zulu. I translated his words for Sir Henry.

"Yes, Umbopa, I will journey there."

"Why do you want to cross the desert where there is no water?" Umbopa asked.

"Tell him," answered Sir Henry, "that I go because I believe that my brother is there. I go

"I'll Reach Him Somehow."

to find him."

Umbopa said, "A person of this village says that a white man went out into the desert two years ago with a guide named Jim. They never came back."

"There's no doubt it's your brother," I told Sir Henry. "I knew Jim well."

"If George meant to cross the desert, he would have done it," Sir Henry said.

"We are much alike," Umbopa said to Sir Henry. "Perhaps I also go to seek a brother over the mountains."

"What do you know of those mountains?" I asked him.

"There is a strange land there," Umbopa said. "A land of witchcraft. But why talk of such things? If we ever get across the mountains, I will tell you more."

He turned back toward the village.

"He knows more than he's saying," I said.

The next day we prepared to start. We couldn't carry our heavy elephant rifles across the desert. We left them and my whip and much of the rest of our gear with a man in the village. Every ounce of weight would slow us down as we crossed the burning sands. We each took a metal water bottle and a blanket. We carried dried meat to eat.

We hired three villagers to go with us for the first day's journey, each carrying a large gourd with a gallon of water. We would then be able to refill our water bottles before we continued.

We waited until after the sun went down. We planned to travel by night, when it would be cooler. We started out just as the moon rose, flooding the country with silver light.

Before we left we stood together looking at the vast desert.

"Gentlemen," Sir Henry said, "we are starting on about as strange a journey as men can make in this world. It is doubtful we will succeed. But we will stand together until the last, no matter what happens."

We all said a silent prayer together. "And now," said Sir Henry, "let's go!"

So we started.

We Walked Through the Moonlit Night.

We had nothing to guide us but the distant mountains and the map that old Jose Silvestre had drawn so long ago. We knew that we had to find the pool of bad water marked on that map or we would die of thirst. And that pool may have dried up many years ago. We had no way of knowing.

As a sailor, Good knew well how to read a compass. He went first and we moved along in single file behind him. We walked along through the moonlit night. When the sun came up we spotted a pile of rocks in the distance and dragged ourselves to it. We climbed beneath a ledge of rock and settled down to escape the heat of the day. We drank some water and ate some of our dried meat.

We slept until three in the afternoon. We drank deeply from our water bottles and refilled them from the gourds. The villagers then headed back while we went on through the lonely wilderness.

It was too dry for any animals. The only living creatures around us were the flies. We walked all night. But this time when the sun came up, we could find no rocks to protect us. By seven o'clock in the morning we were already frying.

"We can't stand this heat for very long," Sir Henry said.

"We'll have to dig a hole," Good answered. "We can climb in and cover ourselves with bushes."

We dug out the sand with our hands until we had made a low hole. We all climbed inside and pulled brush over our heads. This shielded us some from the sun's rays, but the heat was still terrible.

I do not know how we lived through that day. Our water was fast running out. At three in the afternoon we decided it would be better to die walking than to lie there and roast. We each took a little drink and continued.

"We've come fifty miles," Sir Henry said. "We must be near the water marked on the map."

We saw no sign of water. We crept along under the hot sun. When darkness came, we

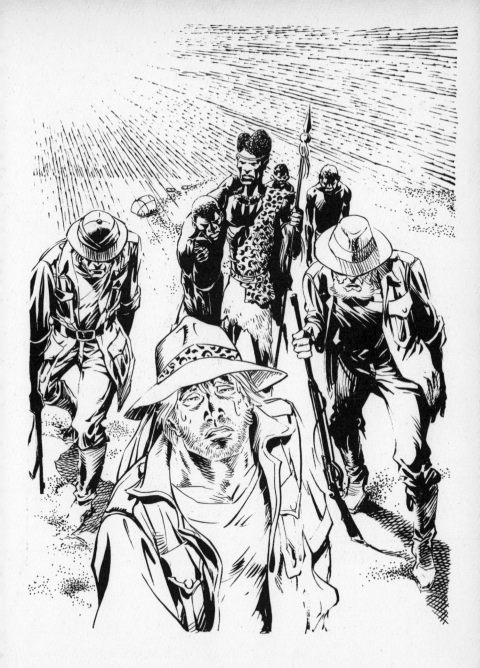

We Dug the Sand with Our Hands.

rested, waiting for the moon to rise. We even slept a little.

Then we moved on, tortured by thirst and prickly heat. We no longer walked but staggered. We barely had the energy left to speak. About two in the morning we arrived at a low hill about a hundred feet high. Here we stopped to rest, drinking down the last of our water.

I was just dropping off to sleep when I heard Umbopa say to himself say in Zulu, "If we cannot find water we shall all be dead before the moon rises tomorrow."

I knew he was right. We must find water or we would suffer an awful death. And soon.

CHAPTER 4

Crossing the Mountains

I woke up at four in the morning, tortured by thirst. I could sleep no more. I had been dreaming that I was sitting in a cool stream with green banks. I awoke to find myself in that dry wilderness. My lips and eyelids were stuck together and I had to rub them open.

Soon the others awoke and we began to discuss the situation. Not a drop of water was left. Our bottles were as dry as bones.

"If we do not find water we shall die," Sir

53

"Fresh Tracks of Antelope"

Henry said.

"Jose Silvestre's map shows water near here," I said. "But where?"

No one had much hope of finding the pool marked in the old map. When it began to get light, Ventvogel rose and walked around the base of the hill with his eyes on the ground. Soon he stopped and pointed to the ground.

"What is it?" we asked. We all ran over to where he was standing.

"Fresh tracks of antelope," he said. "They never go too far from water."

This discovery gave us some hope and renewed our energy. Ventvogel put his nose in the air and sniffed.

"I smell water," he said. We were happy then, knowing there must be water nearby.

At that moment the sun came up, a sight so beautiful that for a moment we forgot how thirsty we were. There, less than forty miles away, were the White Twins, the beginning of the Suliman Mountains. Each peak of the Twins was fifteen thousand feet high. They were connected by a long cliff as if they were the pillars of a gigantic gateway.

There was something solemn and overpowering about those huge mountains, which were certainly extinct volcanoes. The morning light gleamed from their snow-covered tops while white mists gathered around their lower parts.

But soon our thirst became overpowering. It did no good for Ventvogel to smell water if we couldn't find it. We walked all the way around the hill, but found no sign of a spring or a stream or a pool.

"You are a fool," I said angrily to Ventvogel. "There is no water."

"I smell it," he said. "It is close."

"It's in the clouds," I said. "Maybe in two months it will rain and wash our dead bones."

"Maybe it's on top of the hill," Sir Henry suggested.

"Impossible," Captain Good said. "Whoever heard of water found on top of a hill?"

"We might as well go up and look," I said.

Umbopa led us up the sandy slope. "Here it

Our Thirst Became Overpowering.

is!" he cried when he reached the top.

We ran to him. There, in a hollow at the very top of the mound, was a pool of water. We didn't care that it was black and nasty-looking. In a second we were all lying on our stomachs and sucking up the water as if it were the nectar of the gods.

We drank and drank. Then we tore off our clothes and sat in the pool, soaking up the moisture. We rose, refreshed, and ate some of our dried meat. Then we settled down in the shade and slept until noon.

We rested near the water all day. We thanked the ghost of Jose Silvestre who had drawn the map. We figured the water must come from some deep spring.

We drank as much as we could and filled our water bottles before we started on our way. That night we covered twenty-five miles and slept in the shade of some ant heaps. The mountains seemed to tower above us.

The next day we reached the lower slope of one of the White Twins. Our water was gone again. There were no streams coming down the mountain, so we would have to wait until we reached the snow to ease our thirst.

We began our long climb up the lava rock, which made our feet very sore. We were soon exhausted. We stopped to rest. Off to the side, along a flat ridge, we saw an area of green growth. Soil had formed among the stone and birds had dropped seeds. But what good did it do us? We couldn't eat grass.

Still, Umbopa wandered over to have a look at this green patch. A few minutes later he returned, dancing and shouting like a maniac. We hoped he had found water.

"What is it, Umbopa?" I shouted.

"Food!" he replied. "Food and water!" He waved something green in his hand.

It was a melon. He had found a patch of wild melons.

We ran to the melon patch and began to eat. They weren't very tasty, but we were glad for the food and the moisture they contained.

We were still hungry. But our luck held. At

I Fired Two Shots.

that moment a flock of large birds was flying over. I grabbed one of the Winchesters and fired two shots into the midst of them. I was lucky to hit one. It weighed about twenty pounds. We built a fire of melon stalks and roasted him over it. We felt much better when we finished our meal.

That night we again moved on, carrying as many melons as we could. The air became cooler and cooler as we moved higher. The mountainside grew steeper. We could only move at about a mile an hour.

That night we ate our last scrap of dried meat. We knew we would have water as soon as we reached the snow line, but now we began to worry about food. Except for the birds, we had seen no living thing on the mountain.

Now the nights were very cold. We struggled up the mountain without food. We began to feel faint and weak. We sucked on snow to satisfy our thirst, but had nothing at all to eat. At night we wrapped ourselves in our blankets. The cold turned bitter.

Now we were walking through deep snow. Night was coming on and the cold wind made us all shiver.

"According to the map, we must be near that cave," Good said.

"Yes," I said, "if there is a cave."

"We'll find it soon," Sir Henry said.

"If we don't, we're all dead men," I answered.

We continued on in silence. Then Umbopa, who was in the lead, said, "Look!"

He pointed to a hole in the snow just ahead. We hurried on. It was the cave, just as Jose Silvestre had described it.

We crawled inside this small cave just as the sun went down. We huddled together wrapped in our blankets and tried to sleep. But the cold kept us awake. We were worn out from lack of food and from the heat of the desert. Now the cold seemed about to kill us.

Hour after hour we sat there shivering. Not long before dawn I heard Ventvogel's teeth chattering away like mad. Then he gave a deep sigh and fell silent. I thought that he had fallen

Walking Through Deep Snow

asleep.

Finally the sun came up and peeped into our cave. We began to stir, all of us but Ventvogel. I shook him, but he wouldn't wake up. He was stone dead and frozen stiff.

Suddenly I heard a shout of fear from Captain Good. We all turned. The sun was coming straight into the cave now. There at the end, about twenty feet away from us, there was another dead man!

CHAPTER 5

Solomon's Road

The sight of that corpse was too much for us. We all scrambled out of that cave as fast as our legs would carry us. Then we halted, feeling rather foolish to be afraid of a dead man.

"I'm going back," Sir Henry said. "That was the corpse of a man. It could be my brother."

We all crawled back inside. Sir Henry moved toward the dead man and peered into his face.

"Thank God," he said, "it is not my brother."

I looked at the corpse myself. It had gray hair and a mustache. It was naked. Around the

"I Know Who It Is."

neck hung an ivory crucifix.

"I know who it is," Captain Good said, looking over my shoulder.

"Who?" I asked.

"Old Jose Silvestre, of course."

"Impossible," I said. "He died three hundred years ago."

"The cold air preserved his body," Good said. "There are no wild animals here to eat him. No doubt his servant found him dead and took his clothes for warmth. Look, here is the sharp bone that he used to draw the map."

"And there's a wound on his arm," Sir Henry said. "That's where he drew blood to use as ink."

It was sad to imagine the lonely death of the ancient explorer.

"We will leave him a companion," Sir Henry said. We moved the body of Ventvogel to the back of the cave and placed it near that of the old Portuguese gentleman. We went out into the snow, glad of the sunshine but still faint with hunger and cold.

We began to move down the mountain. We couldn't see anything up ahead because of the heavy fog that covered the slope.

Finally we broke out of the mist and saw, at the end of a long stretch of snow, a patch of green. A stream was running through the grass. As the mist cleared, we could look on the entire scene. I have never seen anything like what lay before us. Five hundred feet below where we were, lay expanses of fertile land.

To our left was grassland. We could make out many herds of game or cattle wandering there. This territory was ringed by a wall of distant mountains. To our right was an area of rolling hills. There we could see groups of dome-shaped huts.

"Doesn't that map mention Solomon's Great Road?" Sir Henry asked.

I nodded.

"There it is!" he said, pointing a little to our right.

Captain Good and I looked. There, winding across the plain, was a wide road. How strange

We Could See Groups of Dome-Shaped Huts.

to find what looked like a proper Roman road right in the middle of this wilderness.

We climbed down the mountain to the right and soon we stood with the road at our feet. It had been cut out of solid rock and was at least fifty feet wide. Someone had kept it up very well. The odd thing was it seemed to begin there, right in the middle of nowhere.

"What do you make of it, Quatermain?" Sir Henry asked.

I shook my head. It was a mystery.

"I know," Good said. "This road once ran right over the mountains and across the desert. But a volcanic eruption has covered it with lava. On the other side the sand drifted over it."

It was very much more pleasant travelling downhill on this magnificent road with our stomachs full than it was struggling uphill over snow, starved and half frozen. We grew cheerful. This was quite a road. When it came to a deep ravine it passed over smoothly on a bridge of cut stones. At another spot it zigzagged down a cliff. At a third point it passed through a high ridge by way of a tunnel. Inside the walls of this tunnel we could see carvings of figures driving chariots.

"These appear to be the work of Egyptians," Sir Henry said. "Perhaps they were here even before Solomon's time."

All morning we walked along down the mountain. By noon we had come to an area where lovely silver trees grew along the road.

"There's lots of wood here," Good said. "Let's stop and cook some dinner."

We all agreed to this eagerly. We left the road and found a small stream. We collected some dry wood and soon had a nice fire burning. We cut off pieces of the antelope meat we had brought and roasted them over the fire on the ends of sharp sticks. We ate hungrily and sat down to rest.

The stream flowed gently beside us. After all we had been through this was like paradise. Captain Good took a bath in the stream. Now he was in his underwear, brushing out his

Twenty Paces Beyond Good

clothes. He polished his boots with a piece of fat from the antelope.

Next he produced a small mirror from his bag and looked himself over. He combed his hair very carefully. Then he felt the ten-days beard on his chin.

"Surely," I thought, "he is not going to try and shave."

But he was. He washed his face and scrubbed it with the fat. Then he produced a small razor and began to scrape at his whiskers. It was a painful process, but he soon cleaned off the right side of his face.

Suddenly I saw a flash of light sail past his head.

He and I both started in surprise. A group of men stood twenty paces beyond Good. They were very tall and wore great plumes of black feathers and cloaks of leopard skin. A younger man of seventeen was in front of them. He had just thrown a shiny knife that barely missed Good.

An older man who looked like a soldier

caught the boy by the arm and said something to him. They came closer.

Sir Henry, Captain Good, and Umbopa had by this time grabbed their rifles and stood ready to shoot. The strange men came on, showing no concern. I realized that they didn't know what rifles were or they would have been more careful. "Put down your guns!" I shouted. I knew that our only hope was to make peace with them. I spoke to the older man.

"Greetings," I said in Zulu, not knowing what language to use.

"Greetings," he replied in an old-fashioned form of Zulu. "Where do you come from? Why are three of you white and the fourth like us?"

He pointed at Umbopa. It was true that Umbopa's size and looks were similar to those of the men before us.

"We are strangers from across the mountains," I said. "We come in peace."

"You lie," he answered. "No one can cross the mountains where all things die. No strangers may live in the land of the Kukuana. It is the

"Put Down Your Guns!"

king's law. Prepare to die, strangers!"

The hands of each of the men went toward large and heavy knives they wore at their sides.

"What does he say?" Captain Good asked me.

"He says we are about to be killed," I answered. I looked around. There was no way out.

CHAPTER 6

We Enter Kukuanaland

Good groaned with fear. As he often did
when he was nervous, he pulled his false teeth
out and let them snap back into his mouth.
Seeing this, all the Kukuanas gave a cry of horror and jumped back.

"It's his teeth," whispered Sir Henry. "Take
them out, Good!"

He did so, slipping them into the sleeve of
his shirt.

The old man was drawn toward Good by
curiosity.

"It's His Teeth," Whispered Sir Henry.

"How is it," he asked, "that the man whose legs are bare, who grows hair on one side of his face, and who has one shining eye, can make his teeth move out of his head and back?"

"Open your mouth," I said to Good. He grinned at them, showing them his empty gums.

The men gasped.

Good turned his head and slipped his teeth back in. He grinned again. The young man who had thrown the knife gave a howl of terror.

"I see you are spirits," the old man said. "Pardon us, oh my lords."

"We grant you pardon," I said, going along with their mistake. "It's true we are spirits. We come from another world. We come from the biggest star that shines at night."

They groaned in astonishment.

"We come to visit and to bless you," I said. "But you welcome us by throwing a knife at the head of him whose teeth come and go. How should we judge the man who would do such a terrible thing?"

"Spare him, my lords," the old man said. "He is the king's son."

"Maybe you doubt our power," I said. "I will show you the magic tube that speaks and you will doubt no longer."

I held up a rifle. On a rock about seventy yards away I spotted a small antelope. I pointed.

"I will kill that buck without moving," I said.

"It is not possible," they answered.

I aimed the rifle. I knew I had better not miss.

Bang! The buck fell dead.

The Kukuana men cried out with terror.

"If you want meat, go and fetch the buck," I said. "I do not speak empty words."

"You are wizards, indeed," the old man said. "We will bring you to the king. I am Infadoos, son of Kafa, once king of the Kukuana people. This youth is Scragga, son of Twala, the great king."

"We are ready to meet your king," I said. "But play no tricks on us or the magic tubes

I Knew I Had Better Not Miss.

will talk with you loudly. Beware!"

They at once took up all of our goods except the guns, which they didn't dare to touch. They even grabbed Good's neatly folded clothes.

"Give me those," he said. "I want to put them on."

Umbopa translated.

"Would the lord cover his white legs from the eyes of his servants?" Infadoos asked. "Have we offended the lord?"

I almost exploded with laughter.

"Look here, Good," Sir Henry said, "you can't put your trousers back on. They want you the way you are, in your underwear."

"Yes," I said, "and with whiskers on one side of your face. If you change they might think we are fakes. They might decide to kill us after all."

Good sighed and marched off in his underwear.

All afternoon we travelled along the roadway. I asked Infadoos who made the road.

"It was made in old times, no one knows who

or when, not even the wise woman Gagool."

"How long have your people been here?" I asked him.

"Ten thousand thousand moons," he said. We settled here and became powerful. When King Twala calls his soldiers, their plumes cover the plain as far as an eye can see."

"Who do his armies fight with?"

"Warriors come from the north," he said. "We slay them. Some years ago we also fought a civil war, our people battling among themselves."

"How did that happen?" I asked.

He told me that King Twala, his older brother, was one of a pair of twins. Twala, the younger and weaker baby, was hidden away. Imotu became king when his father, Kafa, died. But a famine came on the land, and everyone was hungry. The people spoke against Imotu. Then Gagool, the terrible woman, hunter of witches, said that Imotu was no king. Twala is to be king! She led Twala out and showed the people that around his waist

They Went Off Toward the Mountains.

was tattooed a snake, the symbol of the son of a king.

The people were mad with hunger. They shouted for Twala to be king. Imotu came out of his hut to see what was happening. He was followed by his wife and his little son Ignosi. At that moment Twala, his own brother, ran to him and stabbed him through the heart. The people all shouted, "Twala is king!"

"Did Twala kill Imotu's wife and son, too?" I asked.

They ran away, he told me. But no one would give them food. They went off toward the mountains, where they must have died. If Ignosi had lived, he would be the true king of the Kukuana people.

"There ahead is the town where Ignosi and his mother were last seen," Infadoos said. "There we shall sleep tonight, if indeed you people of the stars sleep."

"When we are among the Kukuana," I said, "we do as the Kukuana do."

I turned around to speak with the others and

almost ran into Umbopa. He had been following close behind, listening with great interest to what Infadoos had been saying. The expression on his face was strange, as if he were trying to remember something from long ago.

When we reached the village we saw many soldiers marching out toward us. Sir Henry was alarmed. "It looks like we are in for a warm reception," he said.

"Let not my lords be afraid!" Infadoos said. "These soldiers are under my command. They are coming to greet you."

We went on, but we were feeling quite nervous. Half a mile from the gates of the village was a stretch of land sloping upward from the road. Each company of three hundred men stood in formation, their spears and plumes shining in the sun. By the time we arrived, twelve companies awaited us, three thousand six hundred men.

They were powerful warriors, each more than six feet in height. On their heads they wore black plumes like those of our guides.

Spears and Plumes Shining in the Sun

They wore belts of white ox tails around their waists.

Each carried a shield about twenty inches across—metal covered with gray ox hide. For weapons they had short heavy spears that were not made for throwing but for stabbing. Each man also carried three heavy knives that weighed two pounds apiece. One knife hung at the waist, the other two were fixed to the back of his shield. He could hit a target with these from fifty yards away.

As we passed by, each group of men would raise their spears in the air and roar, "Koom!" This was their royal salute. Then they fell in to march behind us.

"These are the Grays," Infadoos told us. "We call them that because of their gray shields. They are the best of the king's warriors."

The women of the town stood and watched us arrive. They stared at Good's "beautiful white legs," which made him very embarrassed.

Infadoos led us to a comfortable hut and told

us to rest. There were couches of tanned skins to lie on and water to wash with. Soon the villagers came in with food: meat, roast corn and honey.

Infadoos and Scragga came to dine with us. The old man was polite, but I could see that the king's son was growing suspicious. If we ate, drank and slept like men, he may have thought, maybe we were not from another world after all.

"Let's ask them about my brother," Sir Henry said.

"Not yet," I warned. "We won't say anything about that until we see what happens."

King Twala, Infadoos told us, was in the main town, Loo, getting ready for the annual feast. All the warriors would attend and parade before the king.

"We will start for there tomorrow," he said.

We Marched Along King Solomon's Road.

CHAPTER 7

Twala the King

As we marched along King Solomon's Road, the villages became more numerous. Hurrying past us were many thousands of warriors. They were headed toward Loo for the big festival. Among the Kukuanas, every able man is a soldier.

At sunset on the second day we stopped to rest on a hill. From there we could see the town of Loo. It was an enormous place, five miles around, with smaller villages surrounding it. A river ran through the center of the city and beyond was a horseshoe-shaped hill. Sixty or seventy miles away we could see three high snow-capped mountains that jutted up from the plain.

"Solomon's Road ends at those mountains," Infadoos told us. "We call them the Three Witches."

"Why does it end there?" I asked.

"Who knows?" he answered with a shrug. "The mountains are full of caves, and there is a great pit between them. The wise men of old used to get what they wanted there. Now it is where we bury our kings, the Place of Death."

"What did the wise men come for?" I asked.

"You lords from the stars do not know?" he asked suspiciously.

"In the stars we know many things," I said. "I have heard that they came for bright stones and yellow iron."

"I do not know," Infadoos said. "Gagool knows. She is as wise as you are."

When he moved away I said to the others, "That's where Solomon's diamond mines are."

The Three Witches

Umbopa said in Zulu, "Yes, the diamonds are there. You shall have them, since you white men are so fond of toys and money."

"How do you know that, Umbopa?" I demanded.

"I dreamed it," he said, laughing. He walked away.

"He knows more than he is saying," Sir Henry said. "Has he heard anything of my brother?"

"He has asked any Kukuana he could, but they all say no white man has ever been in this country before."

"How could he have reached here?" Captain Good said. "We only got over the mountains by a miracle ourselves."

"I still think somehow I shall find him," Sir Henry said, but his face was sad.

Darkness comes suddenly in the tropics. There is no twilight. We waited for the moon to rise before continuing on to Loo.

We could see the thousands of campfires glowing across the plain. They seemed endless.

Soon we reached the gates of the city. Infadoos gave a password and we crossed the drawbridge. We walked for half an hour through the city of grass huts before we reached the place where we were to stay.

We entered the courtyard and found that a hut had been assigned to each of us. We washed. Women from the village brought us food. We ate and drank. Then we asked that all our beds be brought to one hut. We weren't taking any chances.

Weary from our long journey, we slept until the sun was high. But one of us always kept watch. We were told to get ready to meet the king.

"I would like to get ready by getting my clothes back," Captain Good said. But his trousers had been taken to the king.

We washed and combed our hair. Good even shaved—only the right side of his face, of course. Once we had eaten breakfast, Infadoos came to say that Twala was ready to see us. I decided to give him a gift of one of the light

King Twala Came Out.

Winchester rifles.

We were taken to a very large field surrounded by huts. The largest hut was where the kings lived. The field was filled with thousands and thousands of warriors. They stood like statues, holding their shields and spears.

We seated ourselves on the stools in front of the great hut and waited. The air was dead silent. Eight thousand pairs of eyes were watching us.

Finally King Twala came out of the big hut. He was very tall and wore a tiger-skin cloak. His face was cruel and ugly, with only one eye. He wore a shirt of chain armor and carried a huge spear. On his forehead was an enormous uncut diamond.

Scragga, his son was with him. Beside them crawled a small, withered figure who looked like a monkey.

The king raised his spear and all the soldiers shouted, "Koom!" He did this three times. The sound was like thunder.

In the silence that followed, one of the stiff

soldiers accidentally dropped his shield. It clattered to the ground.

"Would you insult me?" Twala roared. "Scragga, show how you can use your spear."

Scragga stepped forward and thrust his spear through the unhappy soldier. We watched, petrified with horror. Sir Henry started to get to his feet, but I held him back.

"Keep calm," I said. "Our lives depend on it."

The king turned to us and greeted us. He asked us why we had come to his land and from where.

"We come from the stars to see this land," I said.

"He comes from the stars, too?" he asked, pointing to Umbopa.

"Indeed he does," I said. "Do not ask about things too high for you, oh King."

"You speak with a loud voice," he said, laughing. "But the stars are far away. You have seen my power."

"And Infadoos and Scragga have told you of our power," I said. "How we kill from far off."

Scragga Thrust His Spear.

"They have told me, but I do not believe," he said. "Kill one of those men over there and I will know it is true."

"We shed no blood of man except as just punishment," I said.

"I insist," Twala said. "Kill a man or I will not believe your power."

"So be it," I declared. "Walk across there, oh King, and you will be dead before you reach the gate. Or send your son Scragga."

Scragga, who had seen our power already, jumped up and ran to hide in the hut.

Twala frowned. "Bring in an ox," he said.

I told Sir Henry to shoot the ox. I wanted Twala to know that all of us had power.

"I hope I make a good shot," Sir Henry said.

"You have to," I told him. "If you miss, we are done for."

The ox was brought into the compound. Sir Henry took careful aim. Bang! went the rifle. The ox fell dead.

A sound of surprise went up from the thousands of soldiers.

"Surely you tell the truth, white man," Twala said.

"We come in peace, oh King," I said. "Here is a staff that will let you kill as we kill. Only never lift it against a man or it shall kill you." I handed him the Winchester. He took it very gingerly and laid it down.

Now the one who looked like a monkey came forward. This person threw off a furry covering to show the strangest face I've ever seen. It was a woman of great age, shrunken to the size of a child. Her skin was a mass of wrinkles. Her scalp was as bald as the head of a vulture. But her eyes were still alive with fire.

She held out her finger, with a nail an inch long, and touched Twala.

"Listen, oh King," she said in a thin voice. "I see the future. I see much blood. Rivers of blood. I hear soldiers coming from all directions."

This, we figured, was Gagool, the witch doctor of the Kukuana people. She spoke as if in a trance.

"First There Will Be Blood."

"Who raised up the three silent ones?" she asked, pointing toward the three distant mountains. "You don't know, but I know. It was white men! They came for the bright stones. Now these white men of the stars come. They are seeking a lost one. You shall not find him here, oh white men. He is not here. You seek the bright stones. But first there will be blood."

She dragged herself across the ground and pointed her skinny finger at Umbopa. "You are not here for stones or yellow metal," she squeaked. "I think I know you. I smell the blood of you. Yes! Yes, you are—"

Before she could finish she fell to the ground in a fit. She could say no more. Some of the soldiers carried her into the hut.

"Gagool has spoken strange words," Twala said. "Perhaps I should kill you all now."

I laughed. "We are not easy to kill, King. Would you like to be as dead as that ox over there?"

"Do not threaten a king!" he shouted.

"I only speak what is true," I said. "Try to kill

us and see."

He thought for a minute. "Go in peace," he said. "Tonight is the great dance. You will see it. Tomorrow we will decide your fate."

There was nothing we could do but obey. I motioned to the others to follow me, and we filed past Twala. I made no other gesture but to bow my head slightly as I passed him. We would show no fear, but not run the risk of angering him either.

It was a very thin line indeed we had to tread before this strange and bloodthirsty king.

"We Will Decide Your Fate."

CHAPTER 8

The Witch Hunt

When we returned to our hut I motioned Infadoos to come in with us.

"It seems to me, Infadoos," I said, "that Twala is a cruel man."

"It is so, my lord," he agreed. "The land cries out with his cruelty. Tonight you will see. At the great witch hunt no man is safe. If the king fears him or wants his cattle, he will be killed. Perhaps I will die myself. The people are weary of Twala and his cruel ways."

"Why then don't they overthrow him?" I

asked.

"If he were killed, Scragga would reign in his place," he said. "His heart is even crueler than that of his father. It is too bad that Ignosi, our rightful king, is not here to take over the throne."

"How do you know that Ignosi is dead?" said a voice behind us. It was Umbopa.

"What do you mean?" Infadoos asked.

"Years ago, the king Imotu was killed. His wife and his son Ignosi ran away. It is said they died in the mountains. But they did not die. They crossed the mountains and met a wandering tribe in the desert. They travelled many months to the land of the Zulu. When his mother died, Ignosi again wandered. He came to where the white men live and learned their wisdom."

"That is a pretty story," Infadoos said, "but I do not believe it."

"There is more," Umbopa said, "Ignosi worked as a soldier and a servant. He waited many years. Finally he met some white men

"You Are Our True King."

who planned to seek this unknown land. They crossed the burning sand and the high mountains and came here, Infadoos."

"You are crazy to talk this way," Infadoos said.

"I am not crazy!" Umbopa shouted. "I am Ignosi, true king of the Kukuana!"

He stripped off his loin cloth. Around his waist was a tattoo of a large snake.

"Koom!" Infadoos said. "It is my brother's son! It is the king!"

"I am not yet king, my uncle," said Umbopa, or as we now knew, Ignosi. "But with your help and the help of these white men, I will be. I will destroy Twala, who killed my father, and Gagool, who drove my mother away. Will you help me?"

Infadoos knelt before Ignosi and took his hand. "Ignosi, you are our true king. I will be with you until I die."

"And will you white men help me?" Ignosi said. "I will repay you by giving you the shining stones."

"You mistake us," Sir Henry said. I translated for him. "Wealth is good, but we do not sell ourselves for diamonds. You have stood by us and I will stand by you. It will be a pleasure to destroy that evil Twala."

"I like a good fight," Captain Good said. "Only you must let me wear my trousers."

"And what of you, old hunter?" Ignosi said to me.

"Umbopa, or Ignosi, I am a man of peace," I said. "But I stick with my friends. I will back you up. But I do want the diamonds, if we can get them. Now what is the plan?"

"Tonight is the great dance and witch hunt," Infadoos said. "Many will die. There will be anger against King Twala. I will speak to the best of the chiefs and win them over. I will have twenty thousand men on our side. We will come to speak with you after the dance if any of us are still alive."

At that point messengers from the king arrived at our hut. They brought three shirts of shining chain armor and three huge battle

"We Do Not Sell Ourselves for Diamonds."

axes, gifts to us from Twala.

"They are magic coats," Infadoos said. "No spear can pass through them. Wear them tonight, my lords."

He left us to rest until the sun went down. We heard the thousands of soldiers marching to the dance. When the moon came up Infadoos returned with twenty men to escort us to the dance. We wore the armor under our regular clothes. We strapped on our revolvers, took the battle axes, and went.

Again, many soldiers were lined up in the great field.

"Why are they so quiet?" Captain Good asked. I translated his question for Infadoos.

"The shadow of death hangs over them," he answered. "Many will be killed tonight. Even you may die. But if we live our plan may work. The soldiers are angry with the king."

Twala now came out of his hut, along with Scragga and Gagool. Twelve gigantic and savage-looking men armed with spears and clubs came with them.

"All who have evil in your hearts, prepare for judgment!" Twala cried. "Let the witch hunt begin."

Ten old ladies appeared. Their hair was white and their faces painted yellow and white. Snake skins hung down their backs. Each carried a forked wand.

"Go," Gagool said. "Do as I have taught you. Go and find the evil ones."

With a wild yell the women danced through the great mass of soldiers.

"I smell an evil-doer!" one of them screamed. She danced faster and faster. Then she stopped dead and stiffened. She crept toward a soldier and pointed at him, touching him with her wand. Instantly the men on either side grabbed this soldier and brought him forth.

"Kill!" the king said.

One of the king's guards drove his spear through the poor soldier, while another crashed his skull with a club.

"One!" counted Twala.

In a second another soldier was dragged

Gagool Began to Dance Around the Fire.

forward and killed in the same way.

"Two!" Twala said.

He kept counting until a hundred bodies were stretched in the dirt. It was the most awful sight I have ever seen.

Around midnight there was a pause. The witch-hunters seemed to have worn themselves out. But now, to our surprise, Gagool herself began to dance around the fire. She rushed back and forth, chanting. Then she touched a tall man standing in front of a large group of soldiers. All his men groaned because he was their leader. It didn't matter. He was dragged forward and killed.

Gagool continued to dance. She came nearer and nearer to where we were sitting.

"I think she's going to point to one of us," Captain Good said.

"Nonsense!" Sir Henry replied.

But she kept inching closer and closer. Her eyes gleamed at us. No doubt about it, she was going to choose one of us to die. Suddenly she rushed forward and touched Umbopa, who was really Ignosi.

"I smell him out!" she cried. "Kill him! Kill him! He is full of evil. Kill him, oh King!"

We froze in our places. The mad old woman was the equal of the king in evil-doing. Ignosi was one of them, but in all our dangerous adventures, he had more than proven himself. He was one of us as well. We were just a few against the many, but we had to stand by our friend.

"Kill Him! Kill Him!"

CHAPTER 9

We Give a Sign

There was a pause before the executioners grabbed our friend. I spoke up quickly.

"This man is the servant of your guests, oh King," I said. "By the law of hospitality you may not harm him."

"Gagool has smelled him out," Twala said. "Gagool says he must die."

"I say whoever touches him will die!" I shouted.

"Seize him!" Twala ordered.

The fierce executioners moved forward.

"Touch him and the king dies," I said. I covered Twala with my revolver. Sir Henry pointed his gun at the leading executioner. Captain Good was aiming at Gagool herself.

Twala hesitated. "Put away your magic tubes," he said. "I will let him live in the name of hospitality, not because I fear you. Go in peace."

"It is well," I said. "We are weary of slaughter and would sleep."

We made our way back to our huts.

"All that killing makes me feel sick," Sir Henry said.

Good added, "If I had any doubts about joining with Umbopa—I mean Ignosi—they are gone now. I'll be glad to see Twala brought down."

"I am grateful to all of you," Ignosi said.

We sat in silence waiting for Infadoos and remembering the horrors we had seen. It was almost dawn when Infadoos arrived. Six other chiefs came with him. Each of them, he said, commanded three thousand soldiers.

Ignosi Showed Him the Tattoo.

"They wish to see the sacred snake before they join with you, Ignosi," Infadoos said.

Ignosi stripped off his girdle again and showed them the tattoo. He told them the same story he had told Infadoos earlier.

"What do you say?" Infadoos asked them. "Will you rise up against the evil king?"

"Your words are true," said an old warrior with white hair. "But if we rise it will mean much blood. Since Ignosi is under the protection of these white men, let us see their power. Let us have a sign so that our men may have faith in the white man's magic."

They all nodded. What sign could we give them? I translated for the others.

"I think I have an idea," Captain Good said. Sailors always carry almanacs and he got his out now. "Look, tomorrow is the fourth of June. On that day there will be a total eclipse of the sun. 'Visible in Africa,' it says. Tell them we will darken the sun just after one o'clock."

It was a good idea, but what if the almanac was wrong? "These predictions are never

121

wrong," Good said. "For half an hour the sun will be completely dark."

"Let's risk it," Sir Henry said.

"We will give you a sign, great men of the Kukuanas," I told the chiefs. "This day, one hour after mid-day, we will make the sun go out. Darkness will cover the earth."

"If you can do this, we will follow you," the old chief said.

"It will be done," I said.

Infadoos explained that two miles from Loo, up on that horseshoe-shaped hill, there was a fort. His soldiers would wait there. Once we had shown the chiefs a sign we would all go there and make war on Twala.

"It is good," I said. "Now let us sleep and make ready our magic."

The chiefs left. Ignosi turned to me and said, "If you can do this wonderful thing I will repay you."

"Promise me one thing," Sir Henry said. I translated his words. "When you are king you will not kill witches or treat your people cruelly

"We Will Follow You," the Old Chief Said.

as Twala does."

"I promise," Ignosi said. "None will die without judgment."

We ate a big breakfast, not knowing when we would get any more food. We waited. At noon Twala would call us for a dance of the village girls. The most beautiful of them, Infadoos had told us, would be killed by Scragga as a sacrifice to the stone ones who sat among the three peaks beyond.

We dressed, again putting on the shirts of chain armor under our clothes. We took our rifles and ammunition. We went back to the king's hut, not knowing what lay ahead.

The great field was filled not with soldiers but with thousands of Kukuana girls. Twala, Scragga, Gagool, and a dozen guards were also there, along with many chiefs.

"Welcome, white men from the stars," Twala said. "Let the dance begin."

The girls danced around the field. They waved palm leaves and white lilies and sang a sweet song. It was pleasant to watch.

Then they paused and one beautiful young woman danced away from the rest. She moved with more grace than our best ballerinas. When she finished her dance, another took her place. Others followed, one at a time.

"Which is the fairest, white men?" Twala asked.

"The first," I said without thinking. Then I remembered that the most beautiful girl would be sacrificed.

"You are right," the king said. "She is fairest and she must die!"

"She has pleased us, oh King," I said. "Why must she die?"

"The figures of stone in those mountains must have a sacrifice," he said. "If I do not give them this maiden, it will be bad luck for me. Scragga, get ready. Sharpen your spear."

The girl was brought forward by the guards. She screamed and struggled. Scragga pointed his spear at her.

I saw Good reaching for his revolver. "What is your name?" Gagool asked the girl.

"Why Must I Die?"

"I am Foulata," she said. "Why must I die? I have done no wrong."

"The stone ones demand a sacrifice," Gagool said. "Be glad you die by the hand of the king's son."

Captain Good snorted with disgust. The girl sensed that he was on her side. She tore herself away from the guards and ran to him. She flung herself down and grasped his "beautiful white legs."

"Protect me, father from the stars," she cried. "Keep me from these cruel men."

"All right," Good said. "I'll look after you. Get up, there's a good girl." He lifted her to her feet.

"Now is the time for the sign," Sir Henry whispered to me. "What are you waiting for?"

"I'm waiting for the eclipse," I said. "I don't see it beginning."

I decided to take a chance anyway. I said, "Twala, this shall not be. Let the girl go."

"Shall not be?" he cried. He was enraged. "Guards, seize the white men. Scragga, kill the girl."

Sir Henry, Good, and Ignosi stood beside me with their rifles.

"Stop!" I shouted. "If you come one step nearer we will put out the sun and bring darkness to your land."

The men halted. "Liar!" Gagool screeched. "No one can put out the sun. Kill them all!"

I looked up at the sky. I hoped for the sake of all our lives the eclipse would begin soon!

"We Will Put Out the Sun!"

CHAPTER 10

We Prepare for Battle

For a minute I could see no darkening of the brilliant light shining from the sun. But then, just as I was losing hope, I saw a faint rim of shadow appear on the bright disk.

I lifted my hands and began to recite some lines from an old poem I knew. Sir Henry and Captain Good did the same. We were all pretending to cast a spell over the sun.

I heard a deep gasp of fear from the crowd.

"Look, oh King!" I said. "Look, Gagool! We keep our word. The sun grows dark before your eyes."

The sound changed to a groan of terror. Only Gagool was not afraid.

"It will pass," she cried. "I have seen it before. The shadow will pass."

"You will see," I said. To Good, I whispered, "Keep swearing, friend."

The shadow continued to eat up the light. The birds even stopped singing, thinking it was evening. A strange quiet settled on the town.

"The sun is dying!" the boy Scragga yelled. "We shall all die in the dark!" He lifted his spear and drove it with all his force at Sir Henry's chest. But he had forgotten the chain armor shirts that the king had given us and that we wore under our clothes. His blow bounced off. Sir Henry grabbed the spear and stuck it straight through Scragga himself. The king's son dropped down dead.

At that moment all of the girls ran away in wild confusion. Even the king retreated to his hut, followed by Gagool and his guards. In a

Thousands of Soldiers Were Waiting.

minute we stood alone, ourselves and the lovely victim Foulata, along with Infadoos and some of the chiefs.

"We have given you a sign, chiefs," I said. "If you are satisfied, let us take advantage of the darkness and run."

We followed Infadoos. Captain Good led Foulata by the hand. We stumbled through the gloom.

Luckily, Infadoos knew all the pathways in the city. He led us onward for an hour. Then the eclipse began to pass and the light returned. We found ourselves outside the town near a large flat-topped hill. It was shaped like a giant horseshoe, with the open side pointed down a slope toward the town. On top was a fort where thousands of soldiers were waiting.

"I had my men bring your things up here," Infadoos said. One of the things they had brought was Captain Good's trousers. He was delighted and immediately started to put them on.

"Why does my lord cover his beautiful white

legs?" Infadoos said sadly.

Good didn't answer. He fastened his pants around his waist and looked very happy. He is a modest man and never liked walking around in his underwear.

In half an hour nearly twenty thousand soldiers were gathered in the hilltop fort, the best of the Kukuana army. Infadoos called them together and spoke.

First he told about Ignosi's father, who had been murdered by Twala. He pointed out how cruel Twala was. He told about our bringing Ignosi over the mountains. He said they must overthrow Twala and make Ignosi king.

Then Ignosi made a speech. "You must choose," he said. "between me and the cruel Twala. I am your true king. If anyone denies that, let him step forward and I will fight him first."

No one stepped forward.

"If you join me and fight Twala, I will reward you with oxen," he said. "And when I sit on my father's throne, the slaughter of innocent men

"You Must Choose," Ignosi Said.

and women will end. There will be no more witch hunts. You will sleep secure."

He pointed down toward the city of Loo.

"Look," he said. "Twala's messengers go out to gather many soldiers. They will try to crush us. Will you stand with me?"

One of the chiefs lifted his hand and there came the royal salute: "Koom!" It meant all the soldiers accepted Ignosi as leader.

Soon after we sat down to talk to the chiefs. We could see that Twala was gathering a mighty army. We had twenty thousand soldiers, but he would soon have forty thousand. Some of his troops were already patrolling around our fort, preparing for the great battle.

"They won't attack tonight," Infadoos said. "Twala needs time to prepare. We must work to block the paths up to this fort."

We agreed. With all the soldiers helping, we set to work. Wherever there were trails coming up the hill we piled heaps of rocks. We also collected boulders we could roll down on the enemy.

Just before sundown a messenger arrived from Twala. He carried a palm branch to show he came in peace.

"The king says you must surrender now and he will give you mercy!" he declared. "If you don't give up, terrible things will happen to you."

"What mercy will Twala show?" I asked out of curiosity.

"One in ten will die as punishment," he said. "The rest will go free. But the white man who killed Scragga must die. Also he who pretends to be the new king, and the traitor Infadoos must die. These are the merciful words of Twala."

I talked to the others and then said to the messenger, "Go back to Twala, you dog. Ignosi is king of the Kukuana. He will not surrender. By tomorrow Twala's corpse will stiffen in the sun."

The messenger laughed. "You do not frighten

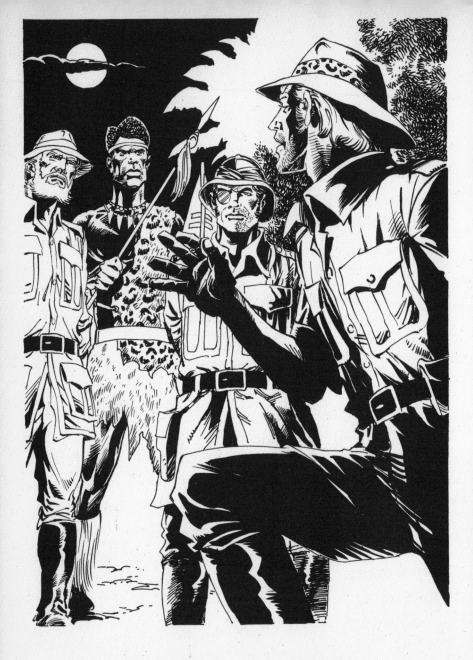

"Luck Goes With the Brave."

me," he said. "You white men will die with all the others. Just wait."

He went back down to the town. Darkness fell over our fort.

We looked out over the thousands of men, their spears gleaming in the moonlight. "I don't think we can hold out against Twala's army," I told Sir Henry.

"It will be a nasty fight, that's sure," he said. "But I would rather die fighting than any other way. Luck goes with the brave. Whatever happens, I'll be in the middle of it."

I think Sir Henry actually liked the idea of fighting. I sure didn't.

Just before dawn we began to prepare. Each of us put on the shirt of chain armor. Sir Henry dressed himself like a native warrior. He wore a leopard-skin cloak and a plume of black ostrich feathers. Infadoos gave him a battle ax and an iron shield like the Kukuana used. Sir Henry also wore his revolver. He made a magnificent sight.

Good and I each carried a spear and a shield, but I certainly didn't know how to use them. We also had our rifles.

After breakfast we met Infadoos and his soldiers, the Grays. This group would wait to be sent where they were most needed once the battle began.

We watched Twala's men streaming out of Loo like columns of ants. One group marched to the right, one to the left. The third came straight toward us.

"They are going to attack us on three sides at once," Infadoos said.

We began to prepare to meet the attack.

We Each Carried a Spear and a Shield.

CHAPTER 11

Twala Attacks

The three columns of Twala's soldiers moved steadily toward us. About a quarter mile away, the middle group stopped to let those on the right and left take up their positions and surround us.

Captain Good, Sir Henry and I took up our rifles and we all began to fire into the masses of soldiers in front. We probably shot ten men before we heard a roar from our right and then from our left. The other groups of enemy soldiers were attacking.

Now they attacked from all directions. Shooting our rifles at them was like throwing pebbles at the waves on the beach. They crashed into our first line of defense shouting "Twala! Twala!" Our men fought back, shouting, "Ignosi! Ignosi!"

The struggle went back and forth. Knives flew through the air. Spears clashed.

They had more men than we did and their troops pushed ours slowly back. Many were killed and wounded on both sides. For a while it seemed as if our men would be defeated.

Sir Henry had been nervously watching the struggle from our lookout point. Now he leaped up and rushed straight into the battle. The soldiers saw his tall figure and shouted, "Here is the Elephant!" They called him the Elephant because he was so big.

Now our men began to fight harder. They pushed Twala's soldiers down the hill. Our troops on the left also defeated their enemy.

We were feeling pretty good when we suddenly saw that on the right our men had been

I Dropped to the Ground in Front of Him.

beaten. Twala's soldiers came running across the top of the horseshoe-shaped hill.

Ignosi issued orders. The Grays, who had not been in the fight, jumped up. Since I was in the middle of them, I had to join them. I hate getting into a fight, but I had no choice.

We charged toward Twala's men. I remember the noise of shields and spears crashing together. I remember a huge Kukuana soldier rushing straight at me with a bloody spear. If I stood where I was, I would be dead. As he came near I dropped to the ground in front of him. He tripped over me and tumbled into the dust. Before he could get back on his feet I shot him with my revolver.

A second later someone knocked me on the head. That was the last I remembered.

When I came to, Captain Good was standing over me with a gourd of water.

"How do you feel, old fellow?" he asked.

I got up and shook myself before I answered.

"Pretty well, thank you," I said.

"When they carried you in, we thought you

were done for," Good said.

"Not this time," I said. "How did the battle end?"

"For now we have pushed them back at every point," he explained. "It was a dreadful struggle. We lost two thousand men, they lost three thousand. Look!"

He pointed to where a long line of soldiers were carrying stretchers made of animal skins. On each was a wounded man. They were brought back to the medicine men, who examined them and treated their wounds as best they could.

I joined Sir Henry, Ignosi, Infadoos and some of the chiefs, who were talking over our plans.

"Thank heaven you're alive, Quatermain," Sir Henry said. "I can't make out what Ignosi wants to do. It looks like Twala means to starve us out."

"It won't take long," Infadoos said. "Our water is almost gone. Before night we will be thirsty. What do you think we should do?"

"What do you say, Ignosi?" I asked.

"Twala Means to Starve Us Out."

"I will give my decision after I hear your advice," he said.

"We have three choices," I said. "We can stay here and starve. We can try to run away to the north. Or we can attack Twala. I think we should attack. We should do it at once, before our wounds grow stiff. If we wait, more troops will join Twala's forces. Even some of our captains may change their minds and switch sides."

Everyone agreed with me. The real decision was for Ignosi to make. He was the king. He thought it over for a few moments. "My heart is fixed," he said at last. "I will strike at Twala. Fortune will decide what happens."

"What plan will we follow?" I asked.

"See how this hill curves around on both sides?" he said. "Infadoos will take his troops, the Grays, and march down the middle into the valley. Twala will send his soldiers to fight the Grays. But they will be protected on the sides by the hills. Twala can attack only in front."

We all looked down the valley to where he was pointing.

"The Elephant, Sir Henry, will go with the first of the Grays. When Twala sees his mighty battle axe he will be afraid. I must stay with the second line. If I were killed right away, you would have no king to fight for."

"It is well, oh King," Infadoos said.

"While Twala's eyes are fixed on this battle," Ignosi said, "part of our men will creep along the hill on the right and on the left. They will charge down onto the sides of Twala's troops and destroy them."

Infadoos went off to prepare the plan of attack. For an hour we all rested and ate our lunch. When it was time to go, I met with Captain Good and Sir Henry.

"Good-bye, you fellows," Good said. "I am going with the troops on the right. I hope we meet again when it is over."

"For myself, I don't expect to see the sun rise tomorrow," Sir Henry said. "I go with the Grays, who will fight to the finish. I hope the

Time for Our Fate to Be Decided

two of you live long enough to get those diamonds."

We all shook hands, not knowing if this was the last time we would see each other. Infadoos led Sir Henry to the lead row of the Grays. I took up my position by Ignosi in the second rank. It was time for our fate to be decided.

CHAPTER 12

The Great Battle

The groups of soldiers who were to attack from the sides moved out along the hill. They would keep out of sight so that they could surprise Twala's troops.

Those of us who would attack in the center got ready. The Grays would go first. I would go with the second group, the Buffaloes, who would back up the Grays if they needed help. Both of these groups were fresh and eager to fight.

Infadoos spoke to his men. He promised that

The Grays Would Go First.

honor and rewards of cattle would go to those who fought bravely. He told them that Sir Henry, the white warrior from the stars, would fight at their side.

I looked at the faces of the Grays. They were brave soldiers. They would have to fight to the death in order to save our army. I knew that most of these men would not return from the battle. But none of them showed fear. They were ready to do their duty.

"There is your king!" Infadoos shouted, pointing to Ignosi. "Go fight and fall for him. Shame will be on the man who shrinks from battle. Let us go and smash Twala's forces!"

For a moment there was silence. Then, like the sound of distant waves, came a sound from all the troops before us. They were tapping their spears against their shields. The sound grew louder. It became a huge noise, echoing off the mountains. Then it slowly died out. All of the soldiers shouted "Koom!" as a salute to the king.

Ignosi lifted his battle axe in reply. The

Grays marched off in three lines. When they had started down the hill, Ignosi put himself at the head of the Buffaloes. I went with them, praying that I would return in one piece.

We could see the Grays ahead of us. They were marching down the grassy slope between the two arms of the hill. Twala's troops were hurrying out to meet them.

The Grays were formed into three lines at the mouth of the small valley. We stood a hundred yards behind them on higher ground, ready to help them if they needed it.

All of Twala's army came forward. But because the space was narrow, only a single group of soldiers could attack. They had to come at the Grays head on.

For a minute, Twala's men stopped. They didn't want to fight the Grays, who were the strongest soldiers of all the Kukuanas.

We could see Twala himself come up and give an order. The first group of soldiers gave a shout and charged up the slope. The Grays didn't move until the attackers were forty

The Crashing Sounded Like Thunder.

yards away. Then they all threw their knives, which rattled against the shields of the enemy.

The Grays gave a terrible shout and sprang forward into the advancing troops of Twala. The crashing together sounded like thunder. The points of the spears flashed in the sun. They fought fiercely. In a few moments, the entire group of Twala's soldiers were destroyed. The Grays lost a third of their men, too. Only two lines remained.

They waited for another attack. I was delighted to catch sight of the yellow beard of Sir Henry among them. He was still alive.

We moved up to the place of the first attack. Dead and dying soldiers lay all around. The ground was soaked with blood.

Now a second group of Twala's soldiers, wearing big white feathers on their heads, came forward. Again the Grays rushed forward to meet them. This time the battle went on for a longer time. The attackers fought furiously. They seemed to be pushing our men back.

We were about ready to move up and help them when we heard Sir Henry's voice shouting above the noise of the battle. He waved his battle axe high. The Grays fought harder. They began to move forward, spearing Twala's men as they went.

"They win a second time," Ignosi said.

Twala's men broke and ran down the slope. The Grays cheered and waved their spears. But now only six hundred of the three thousand remained standing. The rest lay on the ground.

I saw Sir Henry and Infadoos. They chased Twala's troops down the hill. But then another group of fresh enemy soldiers attacked. They surrounded the band of Grays and the fight began again.

I have never liked a fight. I would rather keep my blood inside me. But now, for the first time in my life, I felt an urge to go into battle.

"Why do we just stand here, Ignosi?" I asked. "Our men can't hold out much longer against Twala's troops."

He Waved His Battle Axe High.

"The time has now come," Ignosi said. He lifted his battle axe and gave a signal to his men. Screaming the Kukuana battle cry, we all rushed forward.

I can't tell what followed. I remember a great shouting, a wild clash of spears. We broke through Twala's men and joined the Grays. I found myself standing beside Sir Henry.

Again and again Twala's men charged. Each time we beat them back.

Infadoos was a sturdy old warrior and moved around coolly, giving orders and helping out where the fighting was hardest. Sir Henry also fought well. No one could stand up to the slash of his battle axe. Every time an enemy soldier challenged him he swung. The axe crashed through the other man's shield and cut him down.

Suddenly we heard a cry, "Twala! Twala!" There was the huge one-eyed king himself. He also wore chain armor and carried a battle axe.

"Where is the white man who killed my son

Scragga?" he shouted. "See if you can kill me!"

He threw a knife at Sir Henry. Sir Henry saw it coming and caught it on his shield. Twala leaped forward and swung his axe. It crashed into Sir Henry's shield, knocking him to his knees.

At that moment Twala's troops let loose a shout of surprise. From both sides our men were pouring down the slopes. The troops that had snuck along the hill were now charging.

Twala's men couldn't stand up against the attack. They had already lost many of their troops in battle. Now, attacked on both sides, they turned and ran.

In a few minutes the plain between the hill and Loo was filled with enemy soldiers running away.

But when they had retreated we found that only ninety-five of the Grays still remained. All the rest had been killed.

"This battle will be spoken of by your children's children," Infadoos said. "You have kept your honor, men!"

Twala Swung His Axe.

In the distance we saw one of the last of Twala's men lift his spear and thrust it at Captain Good. Good fell. The Kukuana soldier speared him again and again. We rushed forward, fearing he was dead.

When we reached him he said, "This is excellent armor." Then he fainted. We saw that he had a knife wound in his leg. But the chain armor had saved his life. We placed him on a stretcher and carried him with us.

We joined Ignosi for the march into Loo. We wanted to capture Twala if we could.

At the town Ignosi sent word that he would forgive any soldier who laid down his weapons and surrendered. We marched inside and came to the great courtyard before the king's hut. It was deserted except for Twala himself. He sat there with only Gagool to keep him company. All his friends had left him alone.

"You have defeated my army," he said to Ignosi as we advanced. "What will you do to me?"

"The same that you did to my father,"

Ignosi said.

"A Kukuana king must be allowed to die fighting," Twala said.

"It is so," Ignosi said. "Choose who you would fight. It cannot be me—a king can only fight in war."

Twala looked around with his one eye. What if he chooses me? I thought. I would not fight him for the world.

"I will fight the Elephant," Twala said. "Or is the white man afraid?"

"I will fight with you," Sir Henry said. "You'll see who's afraid."

Twala laughed. As the sun set, each took up a battle axe. They circled around each other.

Sir Henry swung first. He missed and almost fell. Twala brought his axe down with terrible force. But Sir Henry was able to get his shield in the way. They battered each other, each catching the blows on his shield.

The excitement grew. The soldiers shouted and groaned at each stroke. Captain Good recovered and began to cheer for Sir Henry.

They Circled Around Each Other.

"That was a good one!" he said. "Give it to him!"

Sir Henry let loose a massive blow that smashed through Twala's shield, cut his armor, and wounded him on the shoulder. Twala yelled in pain and struck back. His blow cut through the handle of Sir Henry's battle axe and struck him in the face.

Twala leaped toward Sir Henry, who had no weapon to protect himself. I shut my eyes. When I opened them, the two men were wrestling in the dirt.

Sir Henry was able to grab hold of Twala's battle axe. The two men fought over it like wildcats. Sir Henry wrenched the axe loose. He jumped to his feet. Twala came at him and thrust a knife at Sir Henry's chest. The chain armor held.

Twala came forward again. Sir Henry swung the axe with all his might. A roar of excitement went up from the troops. The axe cut right through Twala's neck. His head fell to the ground and rolled to Ignosi's feet. His corpse collapsed in the dust.

I took the great uncut diamond from Twala's brow and handed it to Ignosi.

"Take it," I said. "You are now the King of the Kukuanas!"

Ignosi put on the jewel and raised his spear toward his soldiers. They all raised their spears and shouted "Koom! Koom! Koom!"

The battle was over.

We Were All Badly Bruised.

CHAPTER 13

Going to Find the Diamonds

When the fight was finished, some of the soldiers carried Sir Henry and Captain Good into Twala's hut. I joined them. We were all so tired we couldn't stand up. My head was aching from the blow that had knocked me out that morning.

Because we had saved her life, the beautiful Foulata offered to help us, especially Captain Good. When we took off our shirts of chain armor, we found that we were all badly bruised underneath. The armor stopped spears from going through us, but it didn't keep them from hurting. Foulata mixed up a plaster of green leaves that made us feel better.

Good had a hole through the fleshy part of his leg. He had lost a great deal of blood. Sir Henry had a deep cut on his jaw from Twala's battle axe.

But Captain Good knew how to stitch up cuts. He was able to clean out Sir Henry's wounds and his own and close them up. He smeared antiseptic ointment on them and tied them with a handkerchief.

We drank some strong soup that Foulata had made. Then we lay down on the piles of fur rugs.

Even though we were tired, sleep was difficult. Outside the hut we could hear the wailing of women whose husbands, brothers and sons had died in the war. Twenty thousand Kukuana soldiers had been killed. My sleep wasn't peaceful. I kept dreaming about the awful sights of battle.

When we awoke we found that Captain Good

Ignosi Wore the Royal Diamond.

had a high fever. He was light-headed and spitting blood. He must have had an internal injury.

Infadoos came by to see how we were. He said all the soldiers considered Sir Henry to be the greatest warrior in the world. No one else could have fought all day and then killed the great Twala afterward.

"All of Twala's men have pledged their loyalty to Ignosi," Infadoos told us. "Ignosi is now the king of all our people."

Later in the morning Ignosi himself came by. He wore the royal diamond on his forehead. I couldn't help remembering when, as Umbopa, he had come to us months before, looking to join us on our journey.

"Hail, King!" I said.

"I am the king because of the help I received from you three," he said. "I want to thank you."

"What will you do now with Gagool?" I asked.

"I will kill her," he said. "She made the land evil."

"She knows much," I said. "She knows about the Silent Ones in the mountains and about the place where your kings are buried. Most of all, she knows about the diamonds."

"You are right," he said. "I promised I would help you to find the bright stones. I will let Gagool live if she will guide you."

When Ignosi left I checked on Good. He was out of his mind with fever. He remained very ill for the next four days. I think if it had not been for Foulata, who helped nurse him, he would have died.

Ignosi ordered that no one go near the hut so that Good could rest in quiet. Only Sir Henry and I went in to check on him.

On the fifth night of his illness I went as usual. He was no longer tossing and turning. He lay on the cushion very still. I thought he was dead. I began to cry.

"Hush!" Foulata said. "He needs rest."

Moving closer I saw that Good was not dead. He was fast asleep. The worst was over. He would live.

The People Came to Proclaim Him King.

Captain Good quickly regained his strength. Sir Henry told him all he owed to Foulata. Good took me with him to see her so that I could interpret.

"Tell her," he said, "that I owe her my life. I will never forget her kindness."

"But you saved my life," Foulata said. "I am happy to repay you."

A few days later Ignosi held a gathering. All the Kukuana people came to proclaim him king.

He gave each of the Grays who was still alive a present of cattle and promoted each to be an officer in the army. He thanked the three of us personally. "Everyone in my kingdom should treat these white men with respect," he declared.

After the ceremony was over, we asked him if he had found out anything about King Solomon's Mines.

"Three great figures sit in those mountains at the end of Solomon's Road," he said. "Behind them is a cave where our kings are buried.

Inside the cave is a secret room. Only Gagool knows how to enter. I don't know what is in it. There is a legend that many years ago a white man found great wealth in that room. But the woman who led him there betrayed him. He was driven back to the mountains. No one has entered the room since."

"The story must be true," I said. "We found the white man in the mountains, old Jose Silvestre."

"If we can find the room, you can take as many of the bright stones as you want," Ignosi said. "But only Gagool can show it to you. If she will not do so, she will die."

He ordered the guards to bring Gagool into the hut. When they left her there, she collapsed. She looked more like a pile of rags than a person.

"Beware of my magic, Ignosi," she said.

"Did your magic save Twala?" he asked. "I want you to show us the room where the shining stones are."

She laughed. "None but I know," she said.

More Like a Pile of Rags

"And I will never tell."

"If you don't tell, I will kill you," he said.

"You would not dare," she answered. "If you kill me, you will be cursed forever."

Ignosi took a spear and pushed it into the heap of rags until it pricked Gagool's skin. The old woman screamed.

"Let me live!" she said. "I will show you."

"It is well," Ignosi said. "Tomorrow you will go with Infadoos and my white brothers. If you fail, you will die."

"I will not fail," she said. "But evil will touch any man who goes to that place. A white man went there once, led by another woman named Gagool. He died alone in the mountains."

"That was many years ago," Ignosi said.

"Maybe it was my mother's mother who told me about it," she said. "But her name was Gagool, too. You will see. All of you will see the evil that comes to those who enter the Place of Death."

Her laugh brought a chill to my bones. I wanted to find the diamonds, but I wondered even more about the legend of the mines than I did about the jewels and the other treasures that might lie before us. I knew that Sir Henry was even more anxious about his brother than any of us were about the riches or the legend.

We had to press on. Our very natures as men demanded it from us.

Yet, I couldn't help thinking, with a chill that seemed to come from my very bones, of what horrors still lay ahead of us.

Snow-Topped Mountains Looming Over Us

CHAPTER 14

The Place of Death

It took us three days to hike up Solomon's Road to the base of the mountains known as the "Three Witches." Infadoos and Foulata came with us, along with a group of guards who carried Gagool on a stretcher. She muttered and cursed all the way.

At dusk we set up camp for the night. In the morning we stared at the beautiful sight of those snow-topped mountains looming over us. The white ribbon of Solomon's road stretched to the foot of the center peak, about five miles away, and then it stopped.

You can imagine how excited I felt. At last we were getting close to those wonderful mines that men had sought for centuries. Would we have any better luck than old Jose Silvestre? Or his descendent? Or Sir Henry's brother George? Maybe the place really was cursed. We would soon find out.

We kept going faster and faster as we walked along the great road.

"Why do you hurry toward evil?" Gagool said. Her laugh made a shiver go up my spine.

We kept going. At last we came to a huge circular hole at the base of the mountain. It was half a mile around and about three hundred feet deep.

"Do you know what this is?" I asked Sir Henry and Captain Good.

They shook their heads.

"It's a diamond mine," I said. "It's King Solomon's Mine! Look, they used the water from that stream to wash out the diamonds."

This was the pit marked on Jose Silvestre's

"Why Do You Hurry Toward Evil?"

map. The road split in two here and went along
the hole on each side. Big blocks of stone had
been placed along the rim to prevent the earth
from caving in. On the far side we saw three
towering figures. We hurried around to see
what they were.

"These are the 'Silent Ones,'" Captain Good
said as we approached them.

There were three huge stone carvings, each
one twenty feet high. One was of a woman, the
other two men. They all stared down the road
toward Loo. They looked very cruel. The one on
our right had the face of a devil. They sat there
as if they had gazed across the plain forever.

Who had carved them? Who had dug the
huge pit in front of them? Who had made that
great road that led us here? We would have
given anything to know, but those stone men
and woman were not about to tell us.

Infadoos saluted the "Silent Ones" with his
spear.

"Are you ready to enter the Place of Death?"
he asked. "Or will you take some food first?"

Our curiosity burned more than our hunger.

"We will go in at once," I said, "before Gagool changes her mind about guiding us. We will take some food with us."

We packed some dried meat and a few gourds of water into a basket. Fifty feet behind the big statues was a rock wall eighty feet high. Above that rose the huge snow-capped mountain.

The guards put Gagool down. She gave an evil grin and hobbled toward the rock face. We followed her until we came to a narrow doorway that looked like the opening of a mine.

"Now, white men from the stars, are you ready?" she asked. "I am going to show you the bright stones, as you desire."

"We are ready," I said.

"Good! Your hearts must be strong to see what you shall see."

Infadoos told Gagool that he would wait outside. He was not allowed to enter the Place of Death.

"But do not harm these lords," he said. "If a

"I Will Come."

hair of one of them be hurt, you shall die. Do you hear me?"

"I hear," she said. "Don't worry. I only do what the king asks me to. Here is the lamp. Let us go."

She lit an oil lamp and stepped toward the opening.

"Will you come with us, Foulata?" Captain Good asked.

"I am afraid," she said.

"Then give me the basket of food," he replied.

"No, I will come."

Gagool turned and walked down the narrow passage. We followed. It was terribly dark inside. We heard a sound like the rushing of wings. "What's this!" Good said. "Somebody hit me in the face."

"Bats," I said. "Keep moving."

We moved ahead through the dark for about fifty yards. Then the passage began to grow lighter. In another minute we were inside the most wonderful room. It was huge, bigger than the biggest cathedral. Dim light came from far above.

Even more amazing were the enormous and beautiful pillars that ran along the sides of the room. They seemed to be carved of ice. Some of them were twenty feet thick.

"These are stalactites," I told the others. "They've formed over the centuries. Dripping water leaves deposits of minerals."

We could hear the drip, drip, drip of water. Gagool wasn't interested in any it, though. We followed her onward, thinking we could spend our time looking over the beautiful cave when we returned.

At the farthest point of the cave we found a square doorway that looked like the entrance to an Egyptian temple.

"Are you ready to enter the Place of Death?" Gagool asked.

"Lead on," Good said with a smile. We were all trying to act as if we weren't scared. Foulata, though, grabbed Good by the arm for protection.

Tap, tap, tap, went Gagool's stick down the

Enormous and Beautiful Pillars

passage. I could feel the presence of evil in the passage and held back.

"Hurry or we will lose our guide," Sir Henry said.

I moved down the narrow cave about twenty yards more. We came out in a small room which had long ago been carved out of solid rock. The light was very dim here. All we could see was a stone table with a huge white figure sitting at its head and statues the size of men all around it. All but one were white.

When my eyes adjusted to the light, I saw what these figures were. The sight so upset me, even though I'm not superstitious, that I turned and started to run back out the door. Sir Henry grabbed me by the collar.

But then he, too, saw what the figures were and he began to sweat. Foulata threw her arms around Good's neck and screamed.

Gagool only chuckled.

It was a terrible sight. At the end of the table stood a huge human skeleton, fifteen feet high. He held a spear over his head. He seemed to be grinning.

"Good heavens," Good said. "What are these things?"

"Hee! hee! hee!" Gagool laughed. "Evil comes to him who enters the Place of Death. Come and look at the one you killed!"

We moved closer. We were shocked when we saw that the dark figure sitting at the table was the body of Twala himself! His head, which Sir Henry had cut off, rested on his knees. He was covered with a film that was almost like glass.

"Look," I said. "The water is dripping on him. He is turning into a stalactite!"

Now we looked more closely at the other figures. Each had been a man. The long drip of water had enclosed them in white minerals. They had become part of the cave. This was how the Kukuana preserved their dead kings.

We stared in amazement. We could barely make out their faces through the layers of stone. Twenty-seven of them sat side by side at the table, including Ignosi's father.

Gagool Moved Close to the Skeleton.

"They must have been putting their royal dead here for centuries," Sir Henry said.

"That figure of Death is even older," I said, pointing to the skeleton. "It was carved out of a stalactite by whoever made those giant figures outside the mine."

Gagool moved close to the giant stone skeleton and appeared to be offering prayers to it.

"Gagool," I said. I didn't dare speak in more than a whisper. "Lead us to the room where the stones are."

"You are not afraid?" she asked with a smile.

"Not at all," I said.

"Light your lamp," she ordered. We lit another oil lamp. Gagool pointed toward the wall behind the awful statue. "There is the room you seek."

"Don't joke with us," I said.

"I don't joke," she said.

We moved the lamp closer and saw that the rock was slowly rising. It was a door ten feet high and five feet thick. It must have weighed thirty tons. We didn't see how Gagool had opened it, probably by some hidden lever.

This was it, Solomon's treasure chamber. What was inside? We would know in a minute.

In the light of the lamps, I glanced at the faces of my friends. In the flickering shadows, I saw every possible emotion—hope, excitement, fear. Which one would win out over the others when we were once on the other side of the great stone door?

What Was Inside?

CHAPTER 15

We Find the Treasure

I was so excited I began to shake. At last, King Solomon's diamonds!

"Enter, white men from the stars," Gagool said. "But know that another white man reached this country from over the mountains. He, too, was shown the hidden chamber by a woman who knew the secret of the door. That man filled a bag with bright stones."

"What happened to poor Silvestre?" I asked her.

"How do you know his name?" she said. "The

man must have been frightened. He dropped the bag. He ran out with only one stone in his hand. But the king took that one. It is the one that Ignosi now wears on his forehead. The white man died in the mountains with nothing."

"No one has been inside since?" I asked, looking into the dark chamber.

"None," she said. "No one knows the secret but me. No one could find out that secret, even if he searched a thousand years."

She hobbled into the room. "Come, my lords," she said. "Come and see if the stones are here. Come and see if death is here. Ha, ha ha!"

I waited a minute. I didn't want to enter. "Here goes," Captain Good said. "I'm not going to let that old witch scare me."

He went on, followed by Foulata, who was shivering with fear. Sir Henry and I went after them.

The passageway had been carved out of solid rock. We moved down it part way. Then Foulata, who was terribly afraid, said she felt

"I Think It's Full of Diamonds."

faint and could go no farther. She sat down against the wall. We left the basket of food and water with her and continued on.

At the end of the passage was a painted wooden door. It stood open. In front of it lay a goat-skin sack that appeared to be full of pebbles.

"There is the bag the white man dropped," Gagool said.

Captain Good picked it up. "I think it's full of diamonds," he whispered.

"Let's see what else is here," Sir Henry said. He took the lamp from Gagool and continued through the doorway. We went after him.

"This is Solomon's treasure chamber," I said. The little room had been carved out of rock. Along one wall were piled hundreds of elephant tusks. There was enough ivory here to make a man rich for life.

On the other side were stacks of wooden boxes.

"Maybe those are the diamonds," Good said. We hurried to look. The lid of the first box had been smashed, maybe by Silvestre himself. I thrust my hand inside. I pulled out not diamonds but gold coins. They were marked with strange symbols that none of us had seen before. "These must have been used to pay the workmen of the mines," I said. "At least we won't go home empty-handed."

"The old Portuguese explorer must have put all the diamonds into his bag," Good said.

"Not all," Gagool said. "Look in that dark corner. You will find three stone chests, two of them still sealed."

"How do you know these things?" I asked her.

"Some have eyes that can see through rock," she said mysteriously. I told Sir Henry to search the dark corner.

"Good heavens, look here!" he said a minute later.

We hurried to where he was standing. The stone chests were two feet square. Two of them were fitted with stone lids. The third was open.

"Look!" Sir Henry repeated. The bright

"Some Eyes See Through Rock."

sheen almost blinded us. The chest was full of glittering diamonds. Most of them were larger than any I'd ever seen. I gasped.

"We are the richest men in the world," I said.

"If we can ever get them back to civilization," Sir Henry warned.

"Hee! hee! hee!" Gagool laughed. "There are the bright stones you love, white men. Can you eat them and drink them?"

I broke out laughing myself, I don't know why. Sir Henry and Captain Good joined in. We all laughed and laughed, thinking of how rich we would be.

"Open the other chests," Gagool said. "Take all that you want."

We lifted the heavy lids of the other chests. The second was almost full. The third contained only a few diamonds, but they were the biggest ones, some as large as pigeon eggs.

While we were looking at all these jewels, we didn't see Gagool as she snuck out of the treasure room and down the passageway.

"Help! Help!" we suddenly heard Foulata cry.

"Captain Good! The rock falls!"

"Let go of me, girl," came another voice.

"Help, she has stabbed me!" Foulata screamed.

We ran as fast as we could down the passage, carrying the lamp. The stone door at the end was slowly closing down. Foulata and Gagool were wrestling on the floor nearby. We could see that Foulata had been stabbed, but she still held onto the old witch. Gagool struggled like a wildcat.

Then Gagool broke free. Foulata fell. Gagool dove and scrambled under the stone door. But she didn't make it. The door caught her. The thirty tons of stone continued to drop. It slowly pressed her against the rock below. She shrieked and shrieked. Then, with a sickening crunch, the door was shut.

We turned to Foulata. She had been stabbed by Gagool's knife and couldn't live long. She motioned me closer.

"Tell my friend Captain Good," she said, "that maybe I will see him again in the stars.

"We Are Buried Alive!"

I will search them all. Oh!"

"She is dead," Good said. Tears were running down his face.

"Don't let it bother you, old fellow," Sir Henry told him.

"What do you mean?" Good asked angrily.

"I mean that soon we will all join her," he answered. "Don't you see? We are buried alive!"

CHAPTER 16

Buried Alive

Buried alive! Until Sir Henry spoke those words the full horror of what had happened did not come home to us. Now we understood that the only person who knew how to open the door was dead. It was closed forever and we were on the wrong side of it.

Gagool, we saw, had planned this trap from the beginning. She would have been happy to think of us dying of hunger and thirst while surrounded by the treasure we had come so far to find. Maybe somebody had tried the same

We Were on the Wrong Side.

trick on old Jose Silvestre.

For a while we looked desperately for the handle that worked the door. We could find nothing.

"There is no handle," I said. "That's why Gagool was so desperate to escape."

"Well, at least she was punished for her crime," Sir Henry said. "Let's go back to the treasure room."

We took Foulata's corpse and laid it on the floor beside the boxes of coins. Then we sat down by the diamond chests and divided the food that remained. There were only a few bites for each of us, and one quart of water.

After we had eaten a little we examined all the walls of the room, hoping for another way out. "What time is it, Quatermain?" Sir Henry asked.

I looked at my watch: six o'clock in the evening. We had entered the cave at eleven that morning. The lamp was growing dim. We were almost out of oil.

"If we don't return, Infadoos will search for

us," I said.

"He doesn't know how to open the door," Sir Henry said. "Or even where it is. No one knows. There is no hope for us. Many have died in the hunt for treasure. We will, too."

A minute later the lamp flared up, showing us the whole scene: the tusks, the gold, the diamonds. Then suddenly it sank and went out. We sat there in total darkness.

We tried to get some sleep. We were tired, but the thought of the slow death that we faced made sleep difficult. Plus, it was too quiet to sleep. No one can imagine how terrible true silence is. We knew that thousands of feet above us wind swept over the snow-capped peak. But we couldn't hear even a whisper. No sound at all found its way through the solid rock that separated us from the outside.

We were rich, all right. But we would have gladly given all the diamonds for the hope of escape.

"How many matches do you have, Quatermain?" Sir Henry asked.

He Shouted as Loudly as He Could.

"Eight," I said.

"Strike one and let us see the time."

When I lit the match the light nearly blinded us. It was five o'clock. Dawn would be breaking outside.

We ate a little breakfast. I suggested we try shouting to attract attention. Good had a loud voice. He went down by the stone door and shouted as loudly as he could. But that only made him thirsty and we were almost out of water. No one could hear him anyway. He gave up.

We sat down by the useless diamonds. I gave in to my feelings of despair and began to cry. Captain Good did the same. Sir Henry kept his head and comforted us both.

We sat there all day, a day that was darker than the darkest night for us. I lit another match and saw that it was seven o'clock. We ate and drank a little more. Then an idea struck me suddenly.

"How is it," I said, "that there is still fresh air in here?"

"It can't come through the stone door," Good said. "That's sealed tight. It must come from somewhere else or we wouldn't be able to breathe all this time."

"That means there's hope," Sir Henry said.

We had to try and find where the air was coming from. Each of us crawled around the room on our hands and knees for more than an hour. We kept banging into the walls or the stacks of chests. Sir Henry and I found nothing and gave up. Good continued searching.

"I say, you fellows," he said. "Come here."

We scrambled through the dark to his corner of the room.

"Do you feel anything here?" Good asked us.

"I think I feel air coming up from the floor," I said.

"Listen," he said. He stamped on the floor. It sounded hollow!

I had only three matches left. I lit one. We could see that there was a crack in the floor. Set into that section was a stone ring. Our hearts pounded with hope.

A Crack in the Floor with a Stone Ring

Captain Good had a jackknife. He used it to pry up the ring. He pulled on it with all his might. It wouldn't budge.

"Let me try," I said. I tried and tried to lift it. It was no use. The stone wouldn't move.

Sir Henry tried next and failed.

"Let's give it one more effort," Good said. Sir Henry grabbed the ring. I put my arms around his waist. Good put his arms around my waist. On a signal we all pulled at once.

Suddenly there was a sound, a rush of air, and we all fell over on our backs.

"Light a match," Sir Henry said.

I did so. Beneath where the stone had been was the first step of a stone stairway.

I went back to get the food and water. Then I had an idea. I filled all the pockets of my hunting coat with diamonds. I grabbed a few handfuls of big ones from the third chest and stuffed them in too.

"Won't you take some diamonds, you fellows?" I called to the others.

"Hang the diamonds!" Sir Henry said. "I

hope I never see another one."

Good didn't answer. He wasn't thinking about diamonds but about Foulata. He had been very fond of the girl and was sad to leave her behind.

Sir Henry started to walk carefully down the stair. When he reached the bottom he shouted back, "It's a passage. Come on down."

Good and I followed him down. At the bottom I lit another match. The narrow passage ran right and left. Before we could see any more the match burnt my fingers and went out.

"The air blew the match toward the right," Good said. "That means we should go to the left."

We groped along the passage for a quarter hour. We came to place where another passage cut across it. We took that. A third went off in another direction. We kept going like that for several hours, as if we were moving through a maze.

"It must be an old mine," I said. "Maybe this

Our Last Swallow of Water

is where they found the diamonds."

By now we were completely worn out. We sat down to eat our remaining dried meat and drink our last swallow of water. We saw there was little hope of finding our way out.

"Wait a minute," I said. "What's that? I hear a sound."

"By heavens!" Good said. "It's running water."

We began moving toward the distant sound of water. Soon we came near it.

"Yes," Good said. "I can smell it."

Suddenly, with a splash, Good fell in.

"Where are you?" we shouted in the darkness.

A second later he answered. "I'm here. I have hold of a rock."

I lit the last match. We saw a dark mass of rapidly running water. Good was hanging onto a rock in the middle of the stream. Now he let go and paddled as fast as he could. The stream almost swept him away, but he managed to grab Sir Henry's hand. We pulled him onto the shore.

We drank our fill of water and washed our faces. We went back the way we had come. When we came to another passage, we took it.

"All ways are alike here," Sir Henry said. "We can only go on till we drop."

We were so tired already we could hardly walk. We continued on for a long time, groping through the dark without a hope of finding a way out.

We stopped to rest. Suddenly I grabbed Sir Henry by the arm and said, "What's that? Look!"

"What's That? Look!"

CHAPTER 17

Goodbye

"Is my brain going?" I said. "Or is that light I see?"

We stared into the darkness and there, far ahead of us, was a faint glimmering spot. It was so faint we never would have seen it except that our eyes had looked at nothing but blackness for so long.

We pushed on. In five minutes we were sure. It was a patch of faint light. A breath of real live air was fanning us.

Now the tunnel began to narrow. Sir Henry

continued ahead on his hands and knees. We struggled along behind him. Soon we were all crawling. The hole was hardly larger than a fox's burrow. But now it was earth, not rock.

Sir Henry squeezed forward. Would he fit? He struggled and kicked and then he was out. Good and I followed close behind him. Above us were the blessed stars. Our noses breathed the sweet air. Then something gave and we were tumbling over and over through the grass and bushes and wet soil.

I caught on something and stopped. I yelled to the others. Sir Henry was on some level ground below me. He was out of breath but not hurt. We found Good jammed in the forked root of a tree.

We sat down and cried for joy. We had escaped a dungeon that would have been our grave. In the sky, the dawn we never thought we would see was blushing red.

As the light came down the slope, we saw that we were nearly at the bottom of the vast pit in front of the cave entrance. We could see

We Worked Our Way to the Top.

the three big statues peeking over the edge at us. The caves we had passed through were certainly connected to the diamond mine.

We looked at each other. We were all hollow-eyed, dirty, and bruised. The terrible fear we had felt was written on our faces. Captain Good, though, still had his monocle fixed in his eye. Nothing could make him lose that.

For an hour we worked our way to the top, pulling ourselves by grass and roots. Finally we reached the great road opposite the statues. We walked around and found a fire burning.

Before we reached it we saw Infadoos running toward us. "My lords, it is you come back from the dead!" he shouted.

He took us back to the camp, where we ate and drank and lay down to rest. It took us a couple of days to recover our strength. Then we went back into the pit to try and find the hole we had come out of.

We had no luck. Rain had washed away our tracks. The pit was full of fox holes, but none of them went anywhere.

We entered again the stalactite cave and even the Place of Death. We couldn't see any way to open the great stone door. We couldn't even find the door—the wall was solid rock without a seam.

After a while we gave up. I hated to leave behind what was probably the greatest treasure ever discovered in the world. But I don't know whether I would have had the courage to enter, even if the passage had opened before us.

Maybe someday centuries from now another explorer will find his way into Solomon's treasure chest. Or maybe all those sparkling stones will lay undiscovered forever.

"We can't be too disappointed," I told the others as we started back. "Remember, I filled my pockets with diamonds before we started."

"Do you still have them?" Good asked.

"Most of them fell out when I was sliding down the pit," I said. "But I still have a lot. It's enough to make us all millionaires."

A few days later we were back in our old hut

"I Filled My Pockets."

at Loo. Ignosi listened to our story with wonder. When we came to the part about Gagool's
death he called over the oldest man in the city.

"When you were young," Ignosi said, "do you
remember the witch doctor Gagool?"

"I do, my king," the old man said. "When I
was a child she was already very old, very ugly,
and full of evil."

"She is dead," Ignosi announced.

"That is well," the man replied. "She brought
a curse to our land."

"You see," Ignosi said to us. "All of us rejoice
that she is dead. If she had lived she might
have found a way to kill me as she killed my
father."

When we finished telling our story, I said,
"The time has come for us to say goodbye,
Ignosi. You came with us as a servant, we leave
you as a king. Remember your promise to rule
justly and respect the law. You can repay us by
giving us guides to lead us across the mountains."

Ignosi covered his face with his hands before

he answered.

"What have I done to offend my friends?" he asked. "Settle here with me and I will give you anything—houses, cattle, armies to lead."

"We do not want those things," I said. "We go to seek our own place."

"I see," Ignosi said bitterly. "It is the bright stones you love more than your friends. You only want to go back and sell them and become rich."

I laid my hand on his arm. "Ignosi," I said, "when you were wandering in the land of the Zulu and in the land of the white men, did your heart not turn to your native land that your mother told you about?"

"It did," he said.

"That is all we desire," I said. "To go home."

"You are wise," he said. "I am sad to see you go. There is another way across the mountains. My uncle Infadoos will show it to you. Remember how we stood shoulder to shoulder in the great battle. Goodbye forever, my friends."

The next day at dawn we left Loo with

They Threw Flowers at Our Feet.

Infadoos and a group of soldiers. All the streets were lined with Kukuana who waited to see us go. They gave us the royal salute and threw flowers at our feet.

Before we reached the edge of town a pretty young girl ran up and spoke to Captain Good.

"What is she saying?" he asked me.

"She says she has travelled four days to see your beautiful white legs," I said. "She wants to tell her grandchildren about them."

"I'm not showing my legs to anyone!" he replied.

"You must," Sir Henry said. "How can you refuse a lady?"

Good agreed to pull his pant legs up to the knee. When they saw them, everyone pointed and said, "Ah!" He walked that way until we were out of town. Sir Henry and I could hardly keep from laughing.

Infadoos led us on a path to another pass north of Solomon's Road. This one wound down the face of the cliffs beyond the White Twins.

"Out there in the desert is an oasis with plenty of water," Infadoos told us. "It will make your journey through the sands easier."

"This is probably the way that Ignosi's mother travelled across the mountains," Sir Henry said.

When we reached the cliff we said goodbye to our good friend Infadoos. He told us that he would send five guides with us, carrying plenty of food and water. We all shook hands. Good even gave Infadoos a spare monocle. The old warrior clenched it in his right eye and smiled. It was a strange sight, but he was happy.

We made it to the bottom and started across the desert. That night we camped. Sir Henry said, "There are worse places in the world than Kukuanaland."

"Yes," Good said, "I almost wish I was back there."

"All's well that ends well," I said. "But I hope I never again have as close a call as all the close calls we had there."

The next day we struggled our way across

Good Gave Infadoos a Spare Monocle.

the burning desert and camped again. On the third day we came in sight of the oasis. We would reach it by sundown. It was there we would see the strangest sight of all.

But for now, we were just grateful that relief and shelter were within a few minutes' walk. Even with food and water, the trek across the desert had taken all the effort we were still capable of making.

What else might await us there, we couldn't begin to speculate on.

CHAPTER 18

Found

The sound of running water was very sweet to our ears. I was walking in front of the others. I descended into that green glade and came to the bubbling spring.

I rubbed my eyes. Was I seeing things? Across the stream in the shade of a fig tree was a hut. It was built of grass, as most houses are there, but the door was bigger than usual.

"What the dickens can a hut be doing here?" I said to myself.

Then something even stranger happened.

A Man Limped Out.

The door opened and a white man limped out. He was dressed in skins and had a long black beard.

I thought the sun must be making me see things. No hunter ever came to a place like this. He certainly wouldn't settle here.

As I stared, Sir Henry and Captain Good came up.

"Is that a white man," I asked, "or am I mad?"

The man gave a cry and hobbled forward. Before he reached us he dropped down in a faint. Sir Henry leaped to his side and looked closely into his face.

"Great heavens!" he cried. "It is my brother George!"

A second figure came out of the hut. He also gave a cry and ran toward us.

"Quatermain!" he said. "Don't you remember me? I am Jim, the hunter." He fell down and wept for joy.

The man with the beard recovered. He and

Sir Henry shook hands without a word. Whatever they had quarreled about, it was long forgotten.

"I thought you were dead," Sir Henry said at last. "I have been over Solomon's Mountains looking for you."

"I tried to go over those mountains myself," he answered. "But when I got here a boulder fell on my leg and crushed it. I couldn't go on and I couldn't go back."

That evening, George Curtis told us his story. He had started from Sitanda's Village two years earlier. He had heard of the passage up the cliffs and was trying to reach it. When they got as far as the oasis, Jim tried to extract honey from a bee's nest. He accidentally loosened a boulder, which broke George's leg.

Since they couldn't move, they had lived for two years by shooting game that came to the oasis for water. When their clothes wore out they made new ones of animal hides.

"We were thinking that Jim should go and

"I Thought You Were Dead."

get help from the village," George told us. "He was going to start tomorrow, but I had no hope of ever seeing him again."

Sir Henry told his brother all about our adventures. We had to sit up till late at night to finish the story. We showed him the diamonds. "They belong to Quatermain and Good," Sir Henry said. "That was the bargain."

This made me think. Later, after talking with Good, I said to Sir Henry, "There are plenty of diamonds for everyone. If you won't take your share, we will give them to your brother. He suffered as much as any of us trying to get to them. And he needs the money."

Sir Henry agreed.

The trip back across the desert was difficult. We had to help support George, whose leg was very weak. But we managed.

Back at Sitanda's Village we found our guns and baggage quite safe. We continued on, finally reaching my house near Durban. Sir Henry and George and Captain Good returned to England. I stayed in Africa to write my account of what happened, which is now finished.

This morning I received a letter from Sir Henry: "Captain Good is now clean shaven," it read, "with a new coat and a new monocle.

"You must come back, Quatermain. You can buy a little house near us. We won't tell anyone the story of our adventures until you write your account of them. What's more, your son Harry is here. He has gone hunting with us and is a good sportsman. Please come."

I thought about Sir Henry's letter for several hours. I was suddenly homesick for England, my country that I hadn't seen for so many years. And my son, my Harry, my only living relative.

There's a ship leaving for England on Friday. I think I will sail on it. It will be good to see my boy Harry again. And I must see about getting this story printed. I wouldn't trust anybody else to do it.